THE CHRYSALIS

When Margaret Draycott returns from her daughter's wedding she finds her husband packing. With her children wrapped up in their own lives she is completely alone. A new job boosts her confidence, but this is threatened when she falls for the enigmatic Matthew Sayers. Margaret's struggle to come to terms with her new life makes for an unforgettable story of a woman forced to face the truth about herself.

PHYLLIS DEMAINE

THE CHRYSALIS

Complete and Unabridged

LINFORD
Leicester

First published in Great Britain in 1988 by
Robert Hale Limited
London

First Linford Edition
published September 1992
by arrangement with
Robert Hale Limited
London

British Library CIP Data

Demaine, Phyllis
 The chrysalis.—Large print ed.—
 Linford romance library
 I. Title II. Series
 823.914 [F]

 ISBN 0–7089–7274–8

Published by
F. A. Thorpe (Publishing) Ltd.
Anstey, Leicestershire

Set by Words & Graphics Ltd.
Anstey, Leicestershire
Printed and bound in Great Britain by
T. J. Press (Padstow) Ltd., Padstow, Cornwall

1

MARGARET DRAYCOTT stiffened as she heard the letterbox rattle, her eyes darting to the sitting-room door. When no other sound followed, and even Barney didn't stir from his place on the rug, she sighed and got slowly to her feet to collect the evening paper from the mat.

There was no reason to expect Keith home yet, and the old dog would certainly have recognised his master's footsteps; but every minute, since their daughter, Tracy's, abrupt exit from the house earlier, had seemed like an hour. Now, Margaret felt that her nerves would snap if she couldn't talk to her husband soon.

Though she ought to be used to such times as these, she thought wryly. Hadn't every crisis, minor, or seemingly major, occurred when Keith was absent? In the early years, when Ian and Tracy had been little, it had only been Scotland or London, places from where a phone call could bring his reassuring voice. But, lately, Keith had been spending time around Scandinavia, studying their building designs and techniques, and she couldn't have contacted him, even if he hadn't already been on the homeward bound plane.

Glancing at her watch Margaret turned the newspaper's pages, her thoughts on the bombshell Tracy had dropped.

I suppose I ought to have realised there was something when she arrived last night.

When, since she went to college, has she come home except when she had to? But it had been so nice to see her daughter and Margaret had been only too ready to accept that Tracy had had as much of the people in college that she could stand just now.

"They're so juvenile. Especially this

year's intake," Tracy had declared. "I'll swear I was never so immature."

Margaret hadn't bothered to hide her smile. Tracy was barely nineteen.

"We'll be two old fogies together, then. Unless you're planning to meet up with all your old friends?"

"What friends? Those children I used to know? Hardly."

So it had been 'just the two of them', to Margaret's surprise and eventual waryness.

Tracy had hung around the kitchen whilst Margaret prepared their meals; sat draped across her father's armchair whilst Margaret watched TV; and followed her mother from room to room as she made all straight for Keith's homecoming.

By Saturday afternoon, Margaret was feeling decidedly uncomfortable.

"Your father should be on his way by now," she told Tracy as they settled with coffee and cake round the fire. "We'll have a snack now, then it won't matter if Dad doesn't want to eat until later. He often doesn't."

"Oh, I won't be here when Dad gets in. Didn't I tell you?"

The girl's eyes widened innocently, but Margaret knew that nothing had been mentioned. Tracy bit into a wedge of cake. Whatever was on her mind, Margaret decided, it hadn't ruined her appetite.

"I'm catching the six-thirty train. Ross will be on it."

"He's been home, too?" Margaret registered surprise. It wasn't often either of them came up north, but Ross had called in on previous visits. Tracy and he had been friends for some months and the young man had been fitted, if a little jarringly, into the Draycott household, for Tracy's benefit.

Like Tracy he was a product of his age, the archetypal student, as unlike their own son, Ian, as it was possible to be, but then, Margaret always reminded herself, Ian was married, with a small daughter, so perhaps there was reason for the differences.

"Yes." Tracy answered her mother's question, dabbing a finger at the crumbs on her plate.

"Mother, Ross and I are planning to get married."

"Tracy!" Margaret's cry was half-excitement, half-alarm.

So there had been a reason for this sudden visit!

"You mean you're getting engaged?" she asked, carefully.

"Not exactly." Tracy reached for another piece of cake, then seemed to think better of it and the action increased her mother's unease.

"What do you mean, not exactly?"

"Like I said. We're getting married."

"That wasn't what you said. Planning, you said."

"Oh, Mother! What's the difference? Anyway, if you're being pedantic, the planning's over. We've decided."

This was even more than Margaret had suspected.

"Decided? But, you scarcely know each other."

"Ten months is long enough to get to know someone when you're always together," Tracy declared. "Anyway, people don't wait ages these days. And we're not children. We do know what we're doing."

"Tracy, you're not twenty!"

"Ross is twenty-one. I told you. We've decided."

The girl's eyes were mutinous, her teeth clenched, and Margaret recognised the signs. It would be so easy to back Tracy into a corner, a corner from which, to the girl, there would seem no escape. She must tread carefully.

"Well, I don't . . . I suppose if you've made up your minds. When? Have you thought of a date? There'll be a lot to arrange, and it all takes time; the reception, flowers . . . "

"No!"

The single word broke into Margaret's thoughts like a pebble tossed into a pool, and ripples of warning ran through her.

"Tracy, I don't understand, not any

6

of this. Of course, there'll be things to arrange. Just because I'm not quite . . . that I'd rather you waited a year or two . . . . It doesn't alter things, not all we have to do."

Margaret shrugged, helplessly. "For a start, there's Mr and Mrs Cunliffe. We'll have to meet Ross's parents."

"Why?"

"Why?" Margaret's body jerked as if the word had been some missile. "How do you mean? Because it's usual, of course."

"Like orange blossom and the *Voice that breathed over Eden*, I suppose. Oh, Mother! We don't want all that fuss."

"But inviting the Cunliffes here isn't fuss," Margaret protested weakly. "And what do you mean, fuss?"

"Everything you're planning. Bridesmaids and morning-suits and bouquets."

Tracy thrust denim clad legs to the floor and levered herself upright. Standing looking down at her mother she said slowly, "The whole works,

Mother. All that Ian and Janet had. We don't want any of it. Understand?"

Margaret stared up into her daughter's implacable face, but before she could frame a reply Tracy was heading out of the room.

Stunned, Margaret made no attempt to stop her.

How often, over the years, had this scene; or ones very like it; been enacted between them? But today there were no tears and Tracy was walking calmly up to her room. Margaret saw that, just as there had been no noisy outburst, there would be no tearful apology and reconciliation this time. In that, at least, Tracy appeared to have matured.

A little while later, she heard Tracy's returning steps but she didn't look up until the girl spoke.

"I'm going, Mother."

Margaret turned. The girl had an anorak slung over her shoulder, anchored there by the rope handle of her bag. Beside her feet was the bulky holdall she had brought her clothes in.

"Tracy!"

"I did tell you, Mother. I know it's a bit earlier than I meant to leave, but we'd only argue and it wouldn't change anything. I'll wait for Ross's train at the station. Tell Dad. And tell him it's to be at the registry office."

Margaret put out a hand and her lips moved but she couldn't speak, and Tracy didn't give her time to recover.

"Ross and I will come up one weekend to see to things, there'll be no need for you to bother with anything. But, you'd better know, we're getting married, once Ross has sat his exams."

Suddenly Margaret was on her feet, unaware of the movement.

"You can't! Tracy, that's only a few months off, isn't it?"

"Almost two."

"But, Tracy, have you thought? How will it look? What will all our friends say? You *must* have a proper wedding."

Tracy's lip curled. "It will be proper, all legal and binding, even if it isn't all tied up with satin ribbon. As for your

9

friends, time will prove them right, or wrong, depending on how their minds work. I just don't want the wreath and veil bit."

It was that last phrase which finally reduced Margaret to total silence and she watched Tracy close the outer door behind her without moving.

As the silence settled Margaret began to collect the cups and plates, then, moving like an automaton she carried the tray through to the kitchen.

As the hot water splashed into the bowl sending rainbow bubbles to burst against the tiled wall, Margaret thought of the dreams she'd had which had been shattered just as irrevocably.

Ever since Tracy's birth, but more poignantly since Ian had married Janet, Margaret had dreamed of the sort of wedding she would arrange for her daughter. Janet, the only daughter of Charles Banford, had had a wonderful day. If Margaret was honest, she would have said one which verged on the ostentatious.

Charles and Louise were the kind of people who thought everything which cost a lot of money was the best, taste hadn't entered into things, at least not at the expense of opulence.

True, Janet had seemed to enjoy it all and she couldn't really be blamed for the sort of parents she had, Margaret allowed. And she had proved a good wife to Ian and now an excellent mother to little Victoria. What more could any mother-in-law wish for?

Automatically, Margaret tidied the kitchen and moved back into the sitting-room. Tracy's scorn had been all too evident at Ian's wedding, but she had been sixteen then, now she was almost twenty and contemplating her own wedding. Contemplating? She seemed to have got past that stage; way past. It's all decided. She's just announced they are getting married. She wasn't asking, not even telling me. Anger sparked through Margaret.

I bet she'll expect her father to foot the bill! Yet we're to get no say in how the money's spent? It's so selfish! So unfair!

Oh, I wish Keith were home. He'll have to speak to her. She can't get married in this hole-in-a-corner fashion. What will people think?

Margaret's thoughts came to an abrupt halt. Like one of those electronic mice which interpret a maze, her brain registered the obstacle and veered away.

Not Tracy! What was it she'd said? Time will tell? That must mean . . . ?

No, she was simply being perverse. She'd always been that way. Walking on the very edge of the pavement as a toddler; throwing away her maths and science qualifications.

Margaret had never been happy about this art course Tracy was on when she could so easily have followed Keith into architecture. She did have the brains, whatever she liked to pretend.

She was always the same, Margaret decided, her fingers smoothing the newspaper restlessly. Her eyes followed the movements and her breath caught in her throat as she saw the usual weekend gallery of wedding photos. Tears smarted and a hot lump of misery rose into her throat.

Why me? Why should my daughter be so unfeeling, so ungrateful? I've done everything for that girl and now, now, when all I asked was to give her a lovely wedding day, she refuses.

She knew! She's always known how I felt. The tears brimmed over, rolling down her plump cheeks as she struggled not to let go. Keith must tell her. Perhaps she'll agree for him.

Oh, Keith! Where are you? Why are you never here when I need you? She sprang to her feet, the newspaper falling to the floor as she began to pace the room.

You've told me often enough, she addressed the absent Keith. Saying I do too much for them, always worrying about them, but when have you ever been here when I needed you? It's not fair!

A noise in the hall brought her head up, and recognising the sound of Keith's suitcase being dropped she strode to the door.

"Keith!" she cried, flinging it open. "Where on earth have you been? I've been waiting ages."

The smile on her husband's face waned and he eyed Margaret warily as he edged past her. With a nod, which indicated the brief case, rolled newspaper and duty-free carrier-bag, implying she knew quite well where he'd been, he walked across the room towards the drinks' cabinet.

Margaret followed, speaking angrily to his back.

"Keith! I've been waiting, wanting to talk to you."

He glanced over his shoulder, then went on with the task of pouring a drink.

"I'm not late. We only landed an hour and forty minutes ago. I reckon

I've made good time. I left you the flight times, you knew when to expect me," he accused her.

"Yes. Yes, but . . . "

"Well then? What's the fuss?"

"Keith, Tracy's been."

"And?" He lifted his glass to his lips, then asked. "Anything for you?"

His calmness defused Margaret's anger, somewhat.

"No. Keith, you'll have to speak to Tracy."

"Er . . . You hadn't planned to eat yet, had you? Only there's something . . . "

"When do I ever?" Margaret asked, irritably. "I think, by this time, I know the way you like things done when you get back from a trip."

"Yes, yes. You've always been good that way . . . everything . . . right. You know, I've often thought, you ought to think of yourself a bit more these days. Make a life for yourself."

"Take this business of Tracy, whatever it is . . . she's a big girl now."

"She's not twenty."

"Well, isn't that what I'm saying? The children are both grown up. They don't need you. They don't need us."

Keith took a gulp from the glass. "Sure you won't have one? You look a bit . . . It might help."

"Keith? What is it? What's happened?" Margaret suddenly became aware of his unease.

"Nothing! Well, nothing's happened, not happened, exactly . . . I . . . Margaret I've got something to tell you." He spoke quietly, so quietly that Margaret ignored his words, hurrying on.

"Keith, Tracy said . . . "

"No, Margaret, you've got to listen." Keith raised his voice. "I've got to tell you. I've been thinking about this all the way back, all the last fortnight, for longer than that, of course, really. I mean . . . thinking of telling you, this evening, now."

He put down the glass so heavily the liquid ebbed up to the rim, and he reached towards her, clearly meaning to take her hands.

Something in his attitude alarmed Margaret and she folded her arms round her body, trapping her hands against the soft mounds of her breasts.

Keith, startled by the gesture, stepped back a pace. For several seconds they stared into each other's faces, their eyes wary. Then Keith spoke, his voice so quiet that Margaret tilted her head as if she wasn't certain of hearing him.

"I'm not enjoying this, believe me. There isn't any easy way to tell you. All the things I planned to say . . . they're not . . . I, Margaret . . . "

He held out his hands in an odd, almost supplicating gesture.

She heard the rush of air into his lungs as he breathed deeply and his next words seemed to be expelled from his mouth by the force of its exhalation.

"Margaret, I'm leaving you."

There was no immediate reaction from Margaret and Keith's attitude expressed relief that at last the words

17

had been said. When Margaret finally found her voice her words were as calm as his had been explosive.

"You mean another trip? Right away? You're going away, again?"

It was as if she tried to escape the knowledge her ears had brought her.

"No! Yes! Yes, I am going away, but not on business." Keith spoke almost tetchily. "I'm going and I'm not coming back. Margaret, I'm leaving you, — this house, — our marriage, — everything. Now, do you understand?"

"But . . . but you can't!" It was a gasp of disbelief and Margaret sank on to the edge of the settee, her arms still hugging her body, protectively.

"You can't," she repeated, pitifully. "This is your home. You live here. What will you do? Where will you go? Who'll . . . ?

"Oh, I see!"

Her hands fell into her lap, lying there like small, curled, lifeless animals.

"You've met someone. Some young woman, out there." Now her hands

18

waved vaguely, encompassing that world from which he'd come, a world outside the one she knew.

"Yes, I can see how it is. Someone young, attractive, — skinny!"

"No! It's not like that. I've just made up my mind, but it's not some sudden decision, not to go I mean, just to tell you, — that came suddenly.

"I thought you'd begun to realise, too, that things . . . well . . . !"

"Margaret." He dropped to his haunches before her, his eyes clouded with concern and, again, he tried to take her hands, but as before she snatched them away. He stood, moving to pick up the almost empty glass.

"I know you'll find this hard to believe, but I don't mean to hurt you. I'm fond of you, Margaret."

"Fond?" The word was a snarl. "You're supposed to love me. I'm your wife. You always said you did."

Keith turned from the window where he'd been staring out into the garden, hands thrust into his pockets.

"Isn't that the point, — did? The past? Don't you hear what you're saying? You must realise it's been all over for sometime."

"You can't wipe out over twenty-five years just like that. There's the children."

"They're not babies. I keep telling you. They're not dependent on us any longer."

"But what will they think? How will they feel? Their own father?"

"I don't think they'll care very much. They'll have you, like they've always had," he added, a shade bitterly.

"Oh, so Tracy isn't going to mind that there's no one to take her up the aisle? That's typical of you. I'm the one who's always done everything for those children. Now I'm to give her away as well, am I?"

"Give her? Margaret, what is this? Are you saying that Tracy's planning to get married? She's only a child."

"A moment ago she was all grown up. She didn't need you. None of us needed you. Yet for hours I've been waiting for you." Her breath caught on a sob. "You've got to tell Tracy she can't do this. You've got to tell her. I do need you, you see," she ended with a smirk which might have been an attempt at humour.

"You need . . . " Keith began, his face clouding, but then, with an obvious effort he battened down his anger. "What is all this about? Tracy isn't even engaged."

"They've decided to dispense with all that, as with everything else, it seems. She didn't ask if she could get married; she announced she was doing so. And there's to be no church, no reception. No frills, was the way she put it. Oh, Keith, you've got to make her see! You're her father. You can't just go away and . . . Oh, Keith! Where did I go wrong?"

"I don't suppose it's anyone's fault, not just one of us. I've simply — stopped loving you. I didn't notice, at first, then, suddenly. I don't even know if that's the truth, though there wasn't any one moment when I realised it was over. I can *remember* loving you, but it's as if that was someone else, another person. You're different, not the girl I married. She's gone."

Margaret's head shot up, scorn in her eyes. "Of course she has. I'm not a girl any longer. You're not a young man, either, come to that."

Her eyes raked him, searching for the paunch, the thickening jaw line, the coarsened complexion. When she didn't find them, she said, sulkily. "You're going grey and, and you wear glasses to read. Did you expect me to stay twenty all my life?"

"Of course not! It's not that . . . not all of it."

"I've had children, that alters a woman."

"Yes. I'm not blaming you, Margaret. I'm trying to explain. You, — we're different people now. I've changed, perhaps more than you. You've given your life to the children. Look at the

22

way you're upset about Tracy. Does it really matter? Perhaps it's natural for a mother to take it this way, I don't know. I just feel . . . I've changed," he said again, as if he'd discovered some great truth. "That's it, I've changed! My horizons have broadened. It isn't your fault, I suppose, that, all this; the house, the children; is the only life you know. I'm sorry, Margaret. That's all I can say. I'm sorry. I will talk to Tracy, dear. Try to get her to change her mind, to compromise at least. And . . . "

His gaze turned inward and Margaret watched the thoughts she couldn't read chase across his face.

"I'll stay," he said flatly. "Until the wedding is over. I'll give Tracy away, as you want. Make a speech, pay the bills . . . " He clamped his mouth shut as if his tongue threatened to betray him. "Don't worry. I'll be the dutiful father," he added after a moment.

2

THE meal Margaret prepared for the two of them wasn't eaten with any enjoyment and having cleared the dishes she wandered back into the sitting-room, uncertain what to do. Nothing in their lives together had prepared her for Keith's announcement and she wasn't altogether sure if she really believed what she had heard.

But, as she made to sit across from him, Keith got to his feet.

"I've got some notes, a report. I'll go into the other room, it will be quieter. You can watch TV, then."

Margaret didn't answer, sure that if she spoke at all her anger would come rushing out, anger and bewilderment at what had overtaken her. First Tracy, now Keith. This couldn't be happening. Perhaps Keith was sick? He'd come back shortly and tell her he'd been joking? Well, something. But she didn't really believe what she was thinking and when he did open the door, later, she felt herself stiffening, tensing against another expected blow.

All he said was that she was wanted on the telephone. She didn't remember hearing it ring. But then, she hadn't heard anything that had been said on the television, either.

"A Mrs Warburton. Something about Meals-On-Wheels."

He didn't ask for details when she came back but she supplied them, struggling for some semblance of normality, feeling that if she let go now, she would never recover her hold on events.

"I help out Wednesdays and Fridays, but apparently someone's let them down for Monday. I said I'd step in.

"You always do," Keith said quietly and for some reason Margaret felt reprimanded. Later, when she could stand the silence which lay below the noise of the television no longer, she stood up.

"I'm going to bed."

Keith nodded, not taking his eyes from the screen.

"In the circumstances," Margaret added, goaded by his apparent unconcern. "I'll put your things in the spare room.

She waited, hoping he'd say something, — anything. But he simply nodded.

* * *

Next day Keith absented himself from the house for most of the hours of daylight. Playing golf, pottering around the garden, writing, — yet another report she supposed, though he didn't say so.

She tidied the house, and filled the washer with the stuff from his case, plunging them inside the machine in untidy bundles, not trusting herself not to search for evidence of some kind.

As she dished up the evening meal she heard Keith on the telephone to Tracy and, though she couldn't hear clearly, she gathered by his tone that he was laying down the law.

"They're coming up this next weekend," he told her, taking his place at the table.

"She won't budge from the registry idea, but I think you can start planning a small reception. The sooner the better seems to be the general idea, and I agreed to that."

Margaret shot him a look but his eyes avoided hers. Yes, he would agree to that. He can't wait! Well, he can go. I don't care, she cried. But the sound was all inside her. She couldn't voice the words.

She wouldn't allow her mind to dwell on the future once Tracy was married. Instead she filled every moment with thoughts and plans for that wedding. But her feelings spilled over as he spoke of Tracy's compliance.

"Don't you care? I'd have thought a

father would want to give his daughter a good send off."

"She's given in over the reception."

"And that's enough? Of course, it will be cheaper this way. Though what our friends will think, I can't imagine; or rather I can. Perhaps they are used to the selfishness of young people, these days."

"Perhaps." Keith's voice was non-committal.

"That girl should be thankful I can cook, and you, too. At least I won't disgrace us.

"Margaret. Don't go to extremes," he warned. "She did stipulate only family."

It could have been such fun, even doing it all myself, she thought, as the days passed and she transferred batch after batch of baking to the deep freeze. She had always enjoyed cooking, especially when the children were small.

Once Tracy and Ian had left home Keith had decided that he ate too much rich food away from home, and she had had only herself to indulge. Now she found some satisfaction and an easing of her wounds in the preparations.

Ian and Janet, when they heard of the impending wedding, raised amused eyebrows, both at its abruptness and, what they considered, its parsimony. Margaret ignored all Janet's suggestions regarding suitable outside caterers, glad of the tasks which filled her days and sent her tired to bed.

"I can't understand you doing all this work, especially as Tracy won't care. If you order everything, you won't have to worry about jellies setting and sponges rising," Janet smiled.

"I'm not catering with a children's party in mind," Margaret told her huffily. "My buffet will be as professional as even you could wish."

"Oh, Mother, of course! I didn't mean anything. We all love your cooking. Ian's always saying I'm cruel not allowing him cream in sauces and things. But I tell him it's for his own good. By the way, I could give you my diet sheet. You'll want to get something extra smart for the wedding, I expect."

Ian laughed, putting an arm round his mother's waist. "Hey! Leave Mum alone. Mothers are supposed to be plump and cuddly."

"Then you must find me a disappointment."

"Ah, well! You're different. You're you . . . but Mum . . . "

"Ian! Really! But I still say you are making a lot of work for yourself, Mother." Janet protested.

"I don't mind. When Vicky gets a bit older you'll understand. It's natural for a mother to want to do things for a child, even if . . . " Margaret bit off the last words, but no one seemed to notice.

"Spoil them, you mean" Janet nodded.

"Ian's told me how you always used to put him and Tracy first. Made him selfish, I tell him."

"I am not selfish! Mum just pampered

30

us. Which is more than you ever do."

Margaret joined in the ensuing laughter and no one appeared to notice that hers was a little strained. How could she laugh? How could she go through with this? Seeing Tracy married, knowing what she was thinking, how the girl was viewing her own future, could she bear to watch? What would the child say if she told her it might not last?

Twenty-five years we've had. They've not been bad years. Lots of good times. And it is natural to settle down, to become, well — comfortable. But if Keith was comfortable, her conscience pricked, would he be contemplating leaving? He can't mean it! He can't! I won't believe it. It's all some horrible mistake. He was tired after the trip. Perhaps nothing went right. He won't leave. Of course he won't!

But, despite her thoughts, Margaret shopped carefully for her wedding outfit, remembering what Janet had hinted.

"Nothing too 'mother-of-the-bridish'," she told the assistant in the chain store where she normally shopped, but looking along the more expensive rails. "However, I do think that navy and white's always safe, don't you?"

"Slimming, too, Madam. Yes, that looks quite elegant," the woman said, lifting the jacket with its white trimmed, elbow-length sleeves, into place over the polka dotted blouse.

Yet, Margaret, in her heart, wasn't happy about the wedding. Like Tracy said of herself, she was merely going through the motions.

The whole thing was something of a sham, and when the day arrived Margaret wondered again however she was going to get through it. Her head ached after the sleepless night, and her stomach churned with the sherry she'd gulped in an effort to calm her nerves. But, as she joined Tracy in the hall where she was waiting for her father, Margaret managed to smile. Tracy caught at her fingers.

"I'm sorry I can't be more like the daughter you wanted, Mum. And the one you probably deserve," she whispered.

Margaret's smile wavered and her eyes pricked with the tears she dare not shed in case they became a torrent. She wanted to hold Tracy close, as much to hide her own emotion as for the thought that she was losing her daughter. But, even as a child, Tracy had never allowed them to hug or pet her and Margaret kept her distance now.

"You look lovely, dear. I, I only wanted you to be happy. That's all any mother wants. I've always tried to make you happy."

"But Mum," Tracy's fingers tightened, as if she wanted to convey something important. "We make our own happiness. Don't you see that?" she asked, earnestly.

Then Keith came running down the stairs, looking taller and younger in the light grey suit.

"Hey! Give us a twirl," he grinned. "You look great!"

Tracy dropped a curtsy. "Thank you, kind sir. You look pretty nifty yourself. And don't you agree that Mum should come with us? What difference does going in separate cars make? Tell her Dad."

"Well, you know your Mother, Tracy, always the conventional one," Keith replied, making Margaret feel dowdy and old fashioned. "But it is probably the best way, love."

Margaret didn't speak, opening the door and following the driver to the car. Someone had put a vase of flowers on the long polished table, Margaret saw, as she took her place on the row of chairs facing it. The Registrar, a small man, looked even smaller sitting in the carved, high backed chair, reminding her of Ian play-acting when he was a boy.

Ross was waiting, his hair slightly tamed, and wearing a suit, she was glad to see. He smiled at her and she beamed back, grateful for this little bit of normal behaviour.

The whole ceremony was like a rehearsal, she thought. Where were the beautiful words, the music, the tears? Though what good had those words been to her and Keith?

And there would have been tears if only she had dared to let them flow.

There hadn't even been the conventional photographer; only a man with a curious contraption. But, anyway, the guests seemed disinclined to pose, crowding into cars, as if too eager to get to the food and drink to linger to kiss the bride and wish the couple luck.

But it did mean that she and Keith weren't the first back home, to wait in awkward silence for the others.

The reception turned into one of those Sunday lunches they, and their friends, used as a means of fulfilling obligations when a dinner-party would have been inconvenient.

Only the cake, with its white icing

and silver shoes spoke of the day's purpose. But it was Janet who remembered the ceremony.

"The cake! The happy couple must cut the cake. Come along, Tracy. Mother Draycott! And Dad. And where's the groom?"

She ushered them into place, fitting the couple's fingers round the knife handle. She had even unearthed a camera from the depths of her handbag.

"Now, smile, Tracy! Please! Dad, put your arm round Mother."

Margaret swung startled eyes up to Keith's face as he slipped an arm obediently across her shoulders and smiled down at her.

"Speech! Speech!" the watchers called to Ross, but Margaret didn't hear the stumbled words as, for the first time that day, she allowed tears to trickle down her cheeks.

Champagne corks popped and Ross's friends made the customary jokes as the flash bulbs burst.

Tracy struggled to cut through

the cake, her voice rising impatiently grumbling at her new husband's ineptitude.

"Not like that! Press harder! Oh, Mother, it's no use. Whatever did you put in this icing, cement?"

She pulled her hand free, leaving the knife protruding from the cake where she had jabbed it, bad temperedly.

"It's all a lot of nonsense, anyway. I told you I didn't want all this."

"Tracy!" Keith's voice broke through the sudden silence, fragmenting it into slivers of nervous laughter and high-pitched ribaldry.

And Margaret felt his arm tighten ever so slightly round her. Then Janet was taking command once more.

Margaret thought she ought to be grateful to her daughter-in-law as Janet elbowed her way through to call for a speech from Keith.

"You're supposed to say how sorry you'll be to lose Tracy and to say you're glad to be gaining a son," she told him, her eyes teasing. "That's if you don't mind telling lies, Dad."

Roars of laughter greeted this but Keith held up his hand, calling for attention.

"But it is true. I do welcome Ross. I think he's a very brave man to take on my daughter."

He picked up the glass of champagne someone had put before him.

"Margaret, I know, joins me in wishing them every happiness. We two have been married twenty-five years, a little over actually. It's a long time. But I was remembering the day we got married, this morning, recalling how I felt, — I can't speak for Margaret's feelings, of course. Like Tracy and Ross we were starting out on a new life, an adventure, and I expect they are feeling as I did. A mixture of hope and fear. What will the years bring? Well, they brought me Ian and Tracy. I raise my glass to them, and especially Tracy, today. May she and Ross have many happy years to come."

Again Margaret's eyes sought his,

but Keith's face was buried in the champagne glass and she lifted hers, feeling the bubbles tickle her nose as she drank deeply. And along with the bubbles her spirits rose. He had been thinking of their wedding day! How could he have meant what he said that terrible night?

They had been happy on their wedding day; deliriously happy. So much in love it had been like a pain somewhere deep inside her.

Keith's kisses, his tender loving, had eased that pain, bursting that bubble until it had filled her whole being with ecstasy. Suddenly, she turned to Tracy and, forgetting the old embargo, she took the girl in her arms, holding her very close. For a few moments her daughter allowed herself to be hugged before gently easing herself free.

"Thank you, Daddy, and Mum," she whispered under cover of Janet's command to Ian to pour more champagne.

Once the champagne was finished

Tracy and Ross drove away and the rest of the company slowly began to disperse.

When everyone had left Margaret wandered aimlessly through the rooms, emptying ash-trays and gathering plates and glasses. She couldn't erase from her mind the look she'd seen on Tracy's face as she'd stepped back from their embrace. A look of bewilderment, almost as if she had woken from a dream and couldn't believe where she was. She recalled Tracy's words; 'we make our own happiness'. Wasn't this what she wanted then? Wasn't she happy to be getting married, after all?

Margaret felt Keith watching her and turned to surprise a hint of sadness in his face also. This was supposed to be a happy day. Yet none of them seemed happy.

Keith made a move towards her, then shrugged, saying irritably, "Why don't you leave that? You'll tire yourself out."

"Perhaps Janet was right. It isn't as

if Tracy had wanted all this. Perhaps she'd have been happier if I'd let her have her own way."

"It's too late now," Keith cried. "Do stop worrying."

"But, look what she said? Nonsense, she called it."

"Margaret, you know Tracy. It's all an act. She's not really so tough."

"Isn't she? Don't you think so? I don't seem to know her. I never have known what makes her tick, as they say." She sank down on the edge of her chair.

"I'm beginning to wonder if I know anything about either of my children. I've tried to understand them. Heaven knows, I've tried!"

"Perhaps you've tried too hard. you've had this image of what a good mother should be, and you've tried to live up to it. You've moulded yourself into what you thought you ought to be. I suppose lots of women sink themselves in their children's lives, but you ... You've kept nothing of yourself. You're a mother, nothing else. Not a person. Not the real you."

"The real me?" Margaret stared in amazement. "But . . . I am a mother. That *is* me."

Keith sighed, rubbing a hand across his face. "Perhaps you're right."

He swung on his heel. "Look, there's no point in going over all this. No point in worrying about Tracy, or Ian. They've made their own lives. They've done what they wanted to. Now it's up to us to find our happiness."

"If I could only feel sure that Tracy is happy. All this, today, it was because I wanted it; and it isn't as if I enjoyed it much. There was nothing! No depth. No flowers. No emotion. No photo's even . . . "

"There's the video."

"Video?"

"Yes, didn't you realise?"

"Of course! I just didn't think, I was expecting a camera man. But I should have known. That's just what they would do. Everything slick and modern — and soulless."

"Perhaps it's not that. It's probably a more complete, truthful record than any photograph album."

Keith moved towards the television, picking up the cassette he'd put there. The tape whirred as he set it to run to the start. For a moment he stood beside Margaret's chair, watching the programme on the screen as the video raced through the machine.

"I'm going for a shower," he told her as the machine clicked to a stop. "I'll . . . we'll talk later."

He touched the play button and Magaret nodded as the screen became peppered with dots and snatches of colour.

"You watch. It might help . . . make you feel better," Keith said and he reached a hand to her shoulder, touching it fleetingly.

Her eyes shifted from the screen, but he was already striding from the room, and the pictures on the television claimed her attention. Slowly she leaned back against the cushions. The lack of music and pageantry were still noticeable, but now she saw something she had missed. There was emotion. In the way Tracy reached for Ross's fingers. In the tremor of her voice which was highlighted by the silence in the almost empty room. In the glances which the young couple shared and which she hadn't been able to see. Yes, this camera didn't lie.

Margaret felt the ice which had filled her veins all day begin to thaw, and she listened closely to the words being spoken. They were the same words, the ones she and Keith had used all those years ago, bringing back their wedding day with such clarity that she found breathing difficult.

She glanced around as the film ended, half expecting to find Keith sitting there, but he hadn't returned.

The room was almost dark now, the shadows accentuated by the blue glow from the blank screen. She leaned to switch off the set. Surely Keith had finished his shower by now? What was it he'd said? We'll talk? Yet there had been that strange hesitation before the last word. And . . . ?

Her hand went to the place he had touched, ever so lightly, before leaving, and when she heard a noise overhead her eyes lifted to the ceiling.

Keith was up there! In their bedroom! He hadn't been inside that room since the terrible night of his homecoming. What could he be doing there now? Why their old room? She could feel her heart pounding as the import of her thoughts registered.

It had been by his suggestion that she had watched that evocative film. And he had seemed to be aware of how it would be, the detail, the things she had missed in the ceremony. Had he realised that now there was only the two of them? That their lives were beginning anew, just like Tracy's?

Excitement tingled through her as she got to her feet, smoothing down the skirt of her suit and patting her hair into place. She knew she had looked her best today, that the outfit suited her. Several people had commented on it. Had Keith noticed, too?

Crossing the room, she took a last look around before stepping into the hall. Then, her pace increasing with each step, she climbed towards the closed bedroom door behind which she was sure Keith was waiting for her.

"Keith, you were right," she began, stepping eagerly into the room. "It's a lovely film. I hadn't . . . "

Her voice trailed into silence as she caught sight of the open suitcase on the bed. Inside it lay her husband's neatly folded clothes.

"Keith? Keith!"

"I'm sorry, Margaret. I did tell you; and it's best this way. I can't go on living a lie. You'll be all right. You can stay here and I'll send money regularly."

Stunned, feeling icy cold as the euphoria of a minute before ebbed, Margaret watched him fasten the straps on the case. And when he lifted it down, turning to pick up a further one, she simply followed the movements with her eyes, unable to speak. At the door he hesitated.

"I did say . . . after the wedding," he stated, as if in justification. "And it's true, I'll see you want for nothing."

Margaret heard the words, saw the way he avoided her eyes and something snapped.

"You! You! How dare you say such things? Easing your conscience with platitudes and bribes. Yes, bribes! You talk of money, as if that was all that mattered. But I'll be a mother without children, a wife without a husband . . . Don't you understand anything?"

Keith shrugged, taking a couple of steps onto the landing and, galvanised into action, Margaret ran after him.

"Yes, go!" she shrieked, as he moved rapidly down the stairs. "Go! I don't ever want to see you again. Do you hear me?"

He had opened the door, never

turning once to look at her as she raced down into the hall.

"Go! Go!" she screamed, taking the door in both hands and slamming it savagely behind him. But, as the noise of a car reached her she collapsed against the polished wood, crying bitterly.

3

ARMS spread across the panels of the door Margaret sobbed out her distress. Dimly she heard Keith's footsteps down the drive but it was only as the sound continued that she realised that her husband was actually leaving her.

"*And I told him to go!*" She mouthed the words silently yet they thundered in her head. "*Don't ever come back. Go! Go!*"

"Keith!" That word forced itself from her mouth as her hands began to scrabble with the doorknob. "Come back! Come back!"

Still mumbling incoherently, Margaret wrenched open the door and stumbled over the step. There was no sign of Keith and with one wild look around she began to run towards the gate. Here again the mechanics of the fastener delayed her and, her eyes intent upon the task, she didn't notice the blue car standing a little way up the lane. But, as the catch gave and she swung the gate wide, her head lifted to scan the avenue.

"Keith!" It wasn't a shout, though she had meant it to be, and her husband couldn't have heard as he stood stowing the cases into the car's boot, yet his head lifted.

"Keith?" Again Margaret spoke, an enquiring, puzzled thread of sound as she watched him slam down the lid and move to open the car door. The fact that this was the passenger door only registered as the engine sprang to life, and horrified, Margaret watched as the unknown vehicle came towards her.

It took only seconds for it to pass but in those seconds Margaret had time to see the unhappy, half smile on her husband's face, and to register the face of the woman behind the wheel. Pale, small features in which the eyes, fastened determinedly on the road, looked large and very blue; and straight hair smoothed back into a shining swathe which swung across her shoulders as she checked the traffic at the junction. A sound, half pain, half hysteria escaped from Margaret's soul. A blonde! The proverbial blonde! And she hadn't even known the woman existed.

The garden gate creaked as she thrust it away. The door slammed open and shut behind her unnoticed, as like a wounded animal she sought refuge. Climbing the stairs with an effort, limping into the bedroom, she dropped on to the bed, burying her face in the pillow as if to shut out the scene, sobs aching in her throat. She must have slept, though she couldn't remember the hours of oblivion when she surfaced to pain once more.

Her head throbbed and her face was sticky with the salt of her tears. As if all the moisture had drained from her body via her swollen eyes her tongue felt thick, her lips cracked. Levering herself upright she stumbled to the bathroom, conscious now of the chill night air.

The tumbler chattered against her teeth but the water felt like nectar in her fetid mouth. Yet, when it reached her stomach she rebelled against it recalling the alcohol of the previous day.

Only twelve hours? Or maybe less? Her eyes sought her watch, the incongruency of it still being clasped round her wrist, along with a bracelet and the gold chain at her neck, didn't disturb her as she peered at its face.

Returning to the bed she tore off the navy jacket and skirt, tossing them to the floor, angry at their reminder of the wedding day. And wrapping her arms around her shivering body she crawled under the covers, pulling them tightly around her until she lay in a flower-sprigged cocoon.

Gradually, growing warmer, she slept, waking from nightmares in which Keith taunted her as he danced with a woman with yellow hair.

Once it was daylight when she woke and, for a moment, she forgot, her hand stretching to the bed-side clock. But when consciousness flooded back she curled into a ball again, hugging the pain which gnawed, and sobbed herself into amnesia.

Eventually she could escape no longer and as she lay, wide eyed, listening to the sounds from the avenue she heard her own telephone ringing.

For several seconds, even after the noise had stopped, Margaret lay considering whether she should answer it. The question, she realised, was by this time academic, but it served to keep her mind from wandering down those other, too often explored tracks. Yet, as silence returned so did those questions and with an angry movement she thrust aside the bedclothes, plucking her dressing gown from the door and pushing her arms into its sleeves.

The street noises seemed to have

invaded the house, or perhaps just her mind, and Margaret shook her head irritably as she stood indecisively in the hall. She could no longer tell whether she was hungry or thirsty. Like her mental anguish her bodily needs had subsided to a dull ache. She stared at the mail filling the box, unwilling to do anything which might topple this calmness.

Then she gathered the letters and circulars into her hands, sorting them desultorily, her pulse quickening as she recognised her name on one envelope and Keith's handwriting.

Keith had been here whilst she slept? She recalled now the keys on his dressing table; two solitary door keys. Perhaps it was he who had telephoned, unable to get into the house.

Her fingers tore open the envelope, tugging out the sheet of paper whose serrated edge spoke of its origin.

Margaret, she read. *I'm sorry you had to find out the way you did. I never . . .* The last words were scored through and there was nothing more, just the name, — Keith.

Margaret crushed the letter in her hand until it bit into her palm. The drums started up again in her head, a low relentless throbbing which drove her towards the medicine cabinet in the kitchen. Finding the painkillers she'd been prescribed for the migraine attacks she sometimes suffered, she tipped the bottle over her hand, watching as the pile grew, filling the crevices between her cupped fingers.

The sudden jangle of the telephone caused her hand to shake and the pills cascaded, spilling across the table.

Margaret's head jerked upright. Who could it be? Not Keith. That terse note had robbed her of hope.

"Mother? Mother Draycott?" Her daughter-in-law's voice held censure. "Where on earth have you been?"

"Nowhere."

"You mean you've not been out? Then why haven't you been answering your phone? I've rung and rung."

"I don't have to answer it." Pain brought anger. "There's no law which says I must answer, is there?"

"Mother! What is it? Aren't you well?

"I sincerely hope you're not ill," Janet hurried on. "Because I'm supposed to be bringing Victoria over tomorrow. Don't say you've forgotten. You did say you'd have her for the day of the bazaar. Mother?"

Margaret, dragged back to normal life, became conscious of a strange scratching noise and, as she attempted to locate it, she turned from the phone so that only that last, exasperated cry reached her.

"Look, Janet, I can't talk now. I'll call you back sometime . . . later," she gasped, as she identified the noise.

"Barney!" she cried, slamming down the receiver. "Oh, my darling Barney! What have I done?"

She raced across the kitchen, throwing open the door to the tiny utility room and falling to her knees as the old dog pushed against her.

Barney was yelping and whimpering, little sounds of pleasure, as he tried to scramble on to her lap, his tongue licking any part of her within reach.

"Barney! Oh, Barney! I'm so sorry. So very, very sorry. I forgot all about you. How can you forgive me? Are you all right?"

Scooping him into her arms she hugged him fiercely and his tongue rasped dryly across her face catching the salty tears and reminding her of her own thirst.

"Dear Barney. How horrible it must have been." She laughed tremulously. "What a sorry pair we are."

At last she saw the state of the small room and, lowering the old dog gently to the floor she gazed about her.

"Dear God," she groaned, stepping carefully between the remnants of the waste sack Barney had obviously plundered in his search for food.

His bowl was there, and his water dish, both lying, now, against the wall where he must have pushed them in his efforts to glean every drop of food and moisture.

"Oh, Barney," she cried again, her eyes filling with tears as she turned to him. But what she saw brought her to her knees once more. Hearing the distress in her voice and putting his own construction on its cause Barney was flattening himself against the tiles, squirming on his tummy as he pleaded for forgiveness of his crimes.

"Barney! Barney! I'm not cross. You poor thing. Fancy you thinking that."

She lifted him, kissing his silky ears. "You should be cross with me. You should hate me. Come along." She placed him carefully down. "Let's see what we can find you to eat . . . something very special."

A yelp greeted her words and another, even more excited one as she took cooked meat from the fridge and broke it into his bowl.

"Not too much at first," she told him, pouring water into his bowl. "We don't want you to be sick."

Between mouthfuls Barney continued to cast happy glances at her, whimpering each time her fingers caressed him as she crouched beside him. When both bowls were empty Margaret moved towards the sitting room and Barney followed, tail wagging, body squirming, weaving around her legs as if he couldn't bear to let her go.

"You still love me?" There was amazement in his mistress's voice. "You're not angry? You don't even hold it against me that I neglected you. Oh, Barney, I don't deserve your love."

Slowly she sank down on to a chair and tears flowed once more. But now they came easily, without the harsh sobs which had wracked her through the last hours. And when they ceased, of their own accord, Margaret lifted her head and was able to face this room and the memories it evoked. As she rose to her feet she realised that though her head still ached and the knot of misery deep inside might never fully dissolve, she would never again reach the depths of the last days.

Moving into the hall she lifted the phone and dialled Janet's number.

"Mother, are you all right?"

"Janet." Margaret ignored the question. "Why did you ring? What do you want?"

"You promised you'd have Vicky, don't you remember? Tomorrow, whilst I'm helping at the bazaar?"

"Oh, no, Janet, I couldn't possibly do that."

The thought of the child babbling about her granddad, petrified Margaret.

"But, Mother, you agreed. You always have Vicky for me. Really, I don't understand you, Mother."

Maybe it was the repetition of that last word which caused Margaret's temper to snap. She recalled the conversation with Keith, and the way she had defended herself; — *I am a mother. That is me!*

And Keith had answered, meaning so much more; — *Yes, perhaps you're right.*

"No, I'm sorry, Janet. It doesn't matter what I've always done. I can't look after Victoria."

"Besides," she added, old habits dying hard. "I ... I'm going to see the doctor ... tomorrow," she added, and put down the telephone before Janet could argue.

When Ian and Janet arrived that evening Margaret was sitting before the TV. She wasn't watching. She hadn't any real idea what the programme was, but the silence in the house appeared to have grown as the day progressed, until it hovered around her, its tendrils stretching to bring her flesh to a quivering awareness of its presence. She wasn't even reading, though a book lay open beside her; and she was trying her best not to think.

When the doorbell rang her nerves

contracted, scenting danger, and when it rang a second time she gasped with fear as she heard the door open.

Janet's voice sounded over the soft noise of their footsteps.

"I tell you she sounded weird, Ian. She mustn't be well."

"Mother!"

There it was again, the word she had begun to hate, the word with which Keith had condemned her and her purpose for being.

"The TV's on." Ian spoke again and Margaret imagined him looking exasperated and bewildered, and slightly relieved because the sound of the newscaster's voice suggested normality.

Then they were both in the room. Janet facing her, accusingly. Ian smiling slightly.

Janet said, "We thought you might be ill."

"Where's Dad?" Ian asked. "He's not gone away again, surely?"

"Yes."

Ian's eyes flashed to his wife at the

monosyllabic answer. You were right then, the look said, something is up. He moved closer to his mother.

"What is it, Mum? Aren't you well? You do look sort of washy. When did Dad leave?"

Margaret shook her head, feeling limp now the tension had drained away.

"I don't know. What day is it?"

"Day! Mother! How long have you been like this?" Ian bent over, touching her hand.

"Janet, get Mum a hot drink. She's starved through; It must be flu. She's probably running a temperature. "

"No!"

"But, Mother! Take no notice, Janet." Ian waved his wife towards the kitchen, but she didn't move.

"I don't think she's sick. Something's happened, hasn't it? Something to do with Ian's father? He's not been hurt, has he? No," she shook her head, turning to Ian. "We'd have heard if there'd been an accident . . . your

63

mother in this state. It isn't an accident, is it, Mother?"

"Accident? Oh, no! I think he meant it." Margaret's voice sounded almost amused. "Oh, yes! I think your father meant to do it. It was all planned, all worked out; — the car waiting, the video to keep me occupied. He'd even taken his keys off his ring; — the door keys," she explained, nodding vaguely towards the front of the house. "He'd thought of everything, you see. Everything except how I'd feel. Can you believe he didn't think I'd mind? He walks out of my life and doesn't expect me to care? It's funny, isn't it? That's really very amusing."

She started to laugh, but there was nothing pleasant about the sound.

Later, when Janet had administered hot, sweet tea, and Ian had given her brandy, and when both of them had run out of questions though they had received few answers Ian held her close as they got up to leave.

"Ring me, Mother. I'm sure this is

all some mistake. You're overwrought, now. We'll talk later, decide what's to be done."

Hearing his words and seeing the bewilderment in his face, Margaret could almost feel sorry for him. Poor Ian! He had always worshipped his father. He couldn't believe Keith would ever let him down. Deep inside himself he blamed her, Margaret realised.

Janet clearly blamed Keith. The whole male section of humanity didn't rate too high in Janet's estimation, thought Margaret, but that didn't mean she was ready to let Margaret down any too lightly.

"You must pull yourself together, Mother. No man's worth getting into this state over. And it won't do any good. Don't give him the satisfaction, that's what I say."

Though what satisfaction she was referring to she never defined, since Keith wasn't likely to become aware of his wife's reactions.

"I should go to the doctor," were

Janet's parting words. "He'll give you some tranquillisers, I expect."

So Margaret felt forced to go to the surgery the following morning, knowing that Janet would probably check on her. And I could do with some more pills for my migraine after yesterday, she told herself.

It was some time since she'd last visited Doctor Bentley and Margaret was surprised at the changes made to the old fashioned waiting room she recalled. Now it was bright and airy, the faded old notices gone from the newly-emulsioned walls.

There was a receptionist, too, a young woman sitting behind a glass partition which she slid open as Margaret approached tentatively.

"Dr Bentley?" The receptionist answered Margaret's enquiry with a smile. "He's not in this morning. It isn't one of his days. He doesn't come in often now Doctor Sutcliffe has joined the practice."

"Oh, I didn't know. I suppose

Doctor Bentley is getting older. I hadn't thought. I'll come again . . . "

"Doctor Sutcliffe has had a cancellation. I could fit you in after this patient comes out."

"But . . . " Margaret gave up the struggle. Did it matter who wrote the prescription? It might, in fact, be easier to talk to someone who hadn't known Keith and herself for all these years. Perhaps she did need something for her nerves, as Janet had hinted. "Thank you, I'll wait then."

The young woman nodded and Margaret backed towards the row of chairs. Only two were occupied, a strange thing in itself, to Margaret's thinking. But she remembered friends talking of appointment systems and what the receptionist had said, bore out this idea.

Within a few minutes her name was called and she was directed down the corridor. A corridor which hadn't existed when the elderly doctor was in charge. Everything seemed so different, and Margaret tapped nervously before opening the door. A woman sat behind the desk and Margaret hesitated with the door half-open. Had she come to the right room?

"Come in, Mrs Draycott." The dark head lifted and a smile warmed the younger woman's face.

"I, I, . . . Doctor Sutcliffe?"

"Yes. Won't you sit down? We haven't met before. You must be quite a healthy person," she smiled. "It's almost a year since I joined Doctor Bentley."

"Yes. Yes, I am fit . . . well, except for migraine attacks, now and then."

Margaret moved from the door, but remembered and went back to close it. It seemed natural then to take the chair the doctor had indicated.

"Is it the migraine now?" the doctor asked when Margaret didn't speak.

"Yes, no. Well, that as well. I . . . I haven't been sleeping . . . or eating very well," she faltered. "I thought . . . something to buck me up."

Judith Sutcliffe smiled. "Now you're not going to ask me for a tonic. That's what my elderly patients ask for. I'm sure you know there's no such thing."

Margaret found herself smiling back at this frank woman, but still she couldn't say what had really brought her here. She's not much older than Janet. She'll tell me to pull myself together.

The smile left her face and she twisted her fingers nervously.

After a few moments the doctor left her seat, moving towards the window where several pot-plants stood. She picked up a small, brass watering can and directed a fine spray over the leaves. Margaret watched the sunlight glint in the water droplets relaxing slightly against the chair.

Judith Sutcliffe turned to face her.

"Now are you ready to tell me the real reason you came? Take your time. And, believe me," she added, slipping back behind the desk. "Whatever is troubling you I won't tell you to pull yourself together."

"Janet said that." Margaret smiled back. "My daughter-in-law."

The doctor didn't speak but sat back, hands loosely clasped, face calm; and haltingly at first, Margaret spoke of Keith and his going.

"So you see," she said, as she came back round to Janet's advice. "Perhaps you ought to say that."

She waited, expecting the other woman to speak but Judith merely smiled, shaking her head, slowly.

"I do feel . . . disconnected," Margaret blurted, as if she could force the doctor to agree that she needed pulling together. "I feel sort of . . . angry . . . at myself, not Keith. That's strange, isn't it?"

"Not at all!" The other woman spoke briskly. "It's perfectly natural you should feel guilty, whether you've anything to blame yourself for or not. That's why you're feeling strange, disconnected."

"No," Margaret burst out. "It's not

that. I can understand that I might hate Keith, or myself; that I'd be angry even. But I don't. I don't feel anything. Not anything. Not really. I've even stopped feeling sorry for myself. And I can't care what our friends say; not much anyway. And there's little Victoria. Somehow I can't feel upset that she'll miss her granddad. She thought a lot of him. But then, I don't seem to want to see her either, poor little mite. Or Janet. Or any of them. It doesn't seem right, somehow."

Margaret turned her face from the doctor's keen gaze and made a pretence of searching for the car keys in her bag; even starting to get to her feet.

"I don't know why I came," she said. "There's nothing you can do. I don't know what I expected from you."

"Mrs Draycott, don't go. I think I can help."

She waited until Margaret was sitting once more.

"This feeling of detachment, I shouldn't let it worry you. In fact," she smiled. "It mightn't be a bad thing to go along with it, for a time."

"Of course you were right, there is nothing I can do. I can only give you advice."

"Hard work, would help," she said, after a moment. "Keep your mind occupied and send you tired to bed. Exercise too, for the same reasons. Have you a job?"

"No. I haven't been out to work since the children were born. There was never any need." Margaret grimaced. "Of course, there may be now. I haven't thought about finance, yet."

"I should give it some thought, working I mean. Your confidence has taken a knock. It could help if you found there was a job you could do well, feel useful again."

Margaret shot her a look. How had she known that was how it was, that she felt like rubbish thrown into the dustbin?

Doctor Sutcliffe leaned forward, resting her arms on the desk and looking directly into Margaret's eyes.

"A group; women like yourself who are now alone, for one reason or another; they help each other, in practical ways as well as bolstering one another. One can accept things from someone who has suffered in the same way which we wouldn't accept from others. Like your daughter-in-law's advice," she smiled.

Margaret didn't respond, but the doctor pulled open a drawer, reaching out a notebook.

"I have the address where they meet, and the times, I'll jot them down for you."

Margaret waited whilst she wrote, accepting the slip of paper and tucking it into a pocket of her handbag, politely, before getting to her feet.

"I've taken enough of your time. Thank you. I'll . . . I'll think about what you said, the job and things.

"And I do feel better, — for talking," she added. "Thank you, Doctor, thank you."

Doctor Sutcliffe nodded pleasantly. "I'm here if you need me."

The young woman meant well, Margaret thought as she made her way back home. But she didn't understand.

What would exercise or getting a job do for her? Yes, it would tire her, perhaps she would sleep better, but she would still wake to face another day without Keith. A day which held neither meaning nor purpose. A day when she had to question what her life had meant until now.

And what could I do if I decided to try for work? It's twenty-odd years since I worked. The skills I had then have flown.

I can drive. I can chat to the old ladies and men where I deliver meals twice a week. I can chair a meeting of this committee or that. But of what commercial use is all that? I suppose I could take on extra duties. There must be lots of voluntary workers needed. Keith said I wouldn't want for anything, that he'd send money.

Perhaps I should ask Mrs Warburton if she needs more help, she thought, remembering that the next Wednesday the Meals on Wheels committee were to meet at her home.

There was something to be said for Keith's frequent business trips, Margaret acknowledged, as she prepared for the meeting. At least no one would question his absence.

She had toyed with the idea of saying the meeting would have to be held elsewhere, but then it seemed simpler to allow events to take their course. Explanations might be even more harrowing.

"I couldn't tell them, Barney. I just couldn't."

The little dog looked up from his place on the rug, his eyes bright with affection and, impulsively, Margaret lifted him to nuzzle her face against his head.

Barney had been Keith's dog, supposedly, but since she had been the one to feed and exercise him the wise little animal had devoted himself to her. Now she fancied that Barney sensed her loss and his apparent love and concern helped ease her misery. After that first traumatic few days she had risen each morning, impelled by the knowledge that Barney needed her.

As the door bell rang announcing the first visitor she dropped a kiss on Barney's head before putting him into the kitchen.

"I know," she told him, watching the way his ears drooped. "But it won't be for long, and you wouldn't want to get stepped on."

She pulled the door shut reluctantly as the dog laid his head resignedly on its paws. Then, taking a deep breath she went to answer the bell.

The meeting went well, and decisions; what there were to make; seemed to be arrived at amicably. Margaret took little part in the discussions, contenting herself with raising a hand whenever a vote was called for. Though she wasn't altogether sure what she had voted on, simply following Mrs Warburton's lead.

When, at last, the secretary reached the end of the agenda Margaret rose thankfully to bring in the coffee, and instantly talk broke out among the women. Margaret's heart missed a beat when she heard some other woman's name mentioned, disparagingly, knowing that before long she too would be the subject of their gossip. Despite what she'd told the doctor she discovered it would hurt.

She closed the kitchen door behind her, leaning against it for a moment as Barney greeted her, wondering how she could face them all with this knowledge in her mind. Then she heard a noise and felt someone pushing at the door.

"Margaret, can I help?"

She sprang away, moving quickly to switch on the kettle as Kay Warburton entered.

"No, it's all right. Everything's ready," Margaret cried. "I won't be a moment."

But Kay wasn't to be put off. "I'll take the biscuits, shall I?" And she was gone before Margaret could stop her. But not before Barney had divined her intention and darted through to join the others, eager for any treat which might come his way.

Margaret followed more slowly, putting the tray on the table and pouring coffee whilst Mrs Warburton handed round the biscuits. The chatter continued with scarcely a break and Margaret looked around, wondering how soon she could expect them to leave.

A pair of grey eyes met hers and Margaret felt herself flushing. But the woman smiled, a sympathetic, understanding smile, shrugging her shoulders slightly, as if she too found the others somewhat tiresome.

Margaret's lips lifted a fraction before turning to walk across the room where she could gaze out into the garden. Who was the woman? She didn't think she'd met her at any other meeting.

Had anyone even introduced her? She cast her mind back to the arrival of the women.

Mrs Warburton had been well to the fore, then the others had dribbled in, chatting and throwing cursory greetings Margaret's way.

Yes, someone had said something, indicating the stranger but allowing neither of them to do more than acknowledge each other with a nod and a smile.

"Elizabeth Short. Margaret Draycott."

She looks an Elizabeth, Margaret thought, letting the idea slip into her mind and out again as she looked through the window seeing nothing.

It was an indignant yelp from Barney which finally brought her back to the present and she swung round to see Mrs Warburton holding the little dog high above the floor, his legs dangling as he struggled to break free.

"Outside with you," the woman was saying. "That's the place for dogs. He's begging for biscuits," she declared as

Margaret took a step forward.

Fury deprived Margaret of speech for a second, but then she strode forward and snatched the dog from his tormentor.

"Barney doesn't beg. He's not been taught tricks. Anyway, this is his home. He lives here. If you don't like dogs then, I suggest you're the one who should leave, Mrs Warburton."

During the silence which greeted these words the affronted woman straightened herself to her full height, seeming to tower over Margaret.

"I am not used to being spoken to in that fashion, Mrs Draycott."

She was evidently expecting an apology and when Margaret didn't speak she gathered herself huffily.

"I can only conclude that you are not feeling well," she snapped. "But I will certainly take your advice. Goodbye!"

Margaret said nothing, watching her go, her eyes clouded with anger as she nestled Barney against her breast.

After a few moments, during which

the other women muttered and shifted uneasily, they too began to leave, casting anxious glances in Margaret's direction as they whispered their thanks. As the door closed behind them Margaret sank on to a chair, her heart beating wildly. How had she come to do such a thing, to say such a thing? How? She who always agreed because it was easier, less embarrassing? Had she gone out of her mind? Had the last few days turned her brain?

"I must have been mad, Barney." She bent to fondle the dog's head.

"I wouldn't say that. Quite sane, I think, actually."

Margaret sprang to her feet, swinging round to face the woman who stood in the kitchen doorway.

"You . . . I thought everyone had gone. Why? How? . . ."

"I slipped into the kitchen. I hope you don't mind but I thought you might . . . well, like you said to Barney, I don't suppose you often do things like that. Though I don't agree that you were mad, not in the sense you meant."

Margaret found herself answering the glint of humour in the other woman's eyes.

"I hope they'll be kind enough to think I was temporarily unhinged. They probably will when they . . . hear . . . "

Elizabeth Short smiled, apparently ignoring Margaret's remark.

"I think she got all she deserved, didn't she, Barney?" She bent to the dog and Margaret was thankful of the moment to recover.

Looking up again Elizabeth said, "It needed to be said. I suspect something similar had been on the tip of many tongues.

"I say, good for you. Don't you agree Barney? And I suspect some of the others would second that," she grinned.

4

MARGARET pushed open the heavy door and slid through the gap. The leaflet Doctor Sutcliffe had given her had stated that the Women's Self Help Group met in room five and she viewed the man behind the reception desk warily.

"Where did you want, love?" he asked, when Margaret didn't speak.

"Er . . . room five, please."

There was no reaction, the man simply leant forward, pointing down the corridor.

"To the end, then turn right. You can't miss it."

Margaret nodded, hurrying away, certain he must be watching her and wondering. Yet when she glanced back at the corner he was engaged with someone else. She shrugged. If statistics were to be believed, she wasn't really an oddity, she supposed, checking the numbers.

The thought gave her courage to knock and open the door without hesitating when she found it.

There were several women in the room, women like herself; normal, she thought, with a smile.

"Come along in and find a seat."

A woman, sitting before the others called to her and Margaret obeyed.

"I'm Angela," the woman went on. "You'll learn the others' names later. We use first names, it's easier, and friendlier. Just listen if you wish, unless you feel impelled to contribute."

Angela's smile left Margaret, switching to the woman who'd been speaking when she entered.

Her eyes darting from one speaker to the next, Margaret sat, thinking her own thoughts until, all at once, what one young woman was saying penetrated.

"I never see anyone. You know how it is." She appealed to the others and

Margaret found herself nodding along with them. The woman gave a helpless little shrug.

"People have their own lives to live. Didn't I when I was working? And most women do go out to work, even those with quite small children. And as for friends, well, most of them were Joe's too. I'd like to work, but if I could get a job it would be something humdrum; it'd have to fit in with school times and holidays. How many interesting jobs do you find like that?"

Her voice tailed away and the animation which had lit her face as the words poured forth, dissolved. The rest of the group fell silent, too, except for murmurs of agreement.

"Don't tell me to join something," the woman declared suddenly. "I'm in the Parent-Teacher thing, and coming here last week helped. I read, and listen to talks on the radio, but . . . I feel sort of half-alive."

Angela began to speak but Margaret

got in ahead of her.

"You've given up everything, haven't you? Everything of your own?" Margaret's words surprised her as much as they startled the others, and she felt herself blushing. But she held her ground as the woman faced her.

"What do you mean? I've still got my children, my family. I might not have a husband." She flushed and Margaret understood how she was feeling. How long did one need to stop feeling rejected?

"But I have everything else I thought I wanted." The woman said.

"Didn't you have anything which was just yours? Something you really enjoyed, that was part of your life before you married?"

The other woman nodded, the light gradually coming back into her eyes.

"Yes. Oh, yes!"

"Then take it up again. It doesn't matter what it was . . . You did drop it, didn't you?"

"Yes. It seemed . . . I don't know.

There was never time when the children were babies, and then, later . . . I suppose I just didn't bother. Joe and I . . . I didn't need anything when he, before."

"But you do now," Margaret said quietly. "You must take it up again. You just must. Even if you weren't alone . . . Can't we be wives and mothers, and ourselves?" Her glance took in the others. "Surely we can. We don't have to just be a moth . . er." Her voice faltered.

I am a mother, she had told Keith. That is *me*.

"I'm sorry . . . It was just a thought . . ."

Margaret sank back in her seat, her enthusiasm ebbing, her mind closing against the revitalised chatter around her, unaware that the others were taking up what she'd said, developing her argument. All she could think of was that Keith had been right. After they got married, she had sunk everything into her home and family, and in doing so she'd lost herself.

When the group broke for tea Margaret edged towards the door. This wasn't for her. She'd tried. At least she could tell the young doctor that. But if they couldn't help that other woman what could they do for her?

As she passed by Angela she felt a hand on her arm.

"You were right."

"I'm sorry ... "

"No," Angela said. "Don't apologise. That was sound advice you gave Claire. Have you had any experience of counselling?"

The blonde head tilted enquiringly, blue eyes searching Margaret's face with friendly interest. Margaret shook her head.

"Then you should. If you ever want to, get in touch."

Margaret nodded and the other woman smiled. "Good luck," she said.

★ ★ ★

The telephone was ringing as she stepped into the hall and Margaret didn't hesitate, now, before lifting it. But when she heard Tracy's voice her fingers gripped the receiver tightly, her tongue cleaving to the roof of her mouth.

"Mother? Mother, it is you, isn't it? Oh, blast!" Tracy said in an aside. "I think I've got the wrong number. Hello? Is that . . . ?"

"Yes. Yes, it's me, Tracy. Where are you phoning from?"

"Halfway down the M1. Mother, will it be all right if Ross and I come for the night? It'll break our journey back to Birmingham and we'd like a bath and things. Not to mention a meal I haven't cooked. Hey, get me! I'm sounding like an old married woman already. But who'd spend a honeymoon camping? Still it was fun.

"Mother?" she said again, when Margaret failed to make any response. "What is it? Are you sick, or something?"

With an effort Margaret produced a

laugh. "Of course not! You just took me by surprise. Of course you can come. I hadn't expected to hear from you yet. I'd forgotten your honeymoon was almost over."

"Don't say that, Mum. Where's Dad, by the way?"

"Dad?" Again Margaret's brain and voice refused to work clearly. "How do you mean?" she asked, through stiff lips.

"Mother! You really are woolly minded this afternoon. Is Dad in England? Or is he swanning around the Continent? Will we see him?"

"See him? Oh! No, I don't think so. He is away."

"Tough luck!" The pips sounded and Tracy gabbled, "See you around six, then. Bye!"

Margaret held the phone a long time after the line went dead.

She'd have to tell Tracy. How could she do it? What words could she use? For all her outward hardness Tracy loved her father.

She'll think it's my fault! And it's not! It's not! I didn't do anything, Margaret screamed, silently. She dropped the receiver back in place as she heard a faint whine and felt the warmth of a furry body against her legs. Dropping to her haunches she cuddled Barney.

"You know it wasn't my fault, don't you?"

The dog licked her face and whined again and Margaret held him from her, staring into his face.

"What is it, Barney, love?" Her fingers touched his nose. It was dry and hot. "What is it? I don't think you're happy, are you? You miss him, too. Oh, Barney! Don't get sick on me."

"Come along! Supper time!" she said, brightly, turning towards the kitchen. There she spooned meat into Barney's bowl, mixing in a powder unobtrusively. "You'll soon feel better. And I love you. You know I do. Eat up, boy!"

An hour later, Tracy and her husband entered the house like a couple of gypsies, their small, ancient car festooned with items of luggage seeming to cling to the struts of the roof rack. Their bare legs tanned, and Tracy's hair a tangled mass.

"The water's hot," Margaret told them, once the preliminary greetings were over. She had been surprised by the warmth of Ross's hug, and even unemotional Tracy had kissed her cheek, laying her hands on her mother's shoulders and gazing into her eyes briefly.

"I've got a casserole in the oven," Margaret told them, covering the moment when Tracy drew back into herself once more. "But, it will keep. Have a long soak."

"Mother thinks we haven't washed since the wedding day," Tracy grinned over her shoulder at her husband from halfway up the stairs. "Which room have you put us into?"

"Ours." The word was out before Margaret could stop it, but Tracy didn't react.

Later, Margaret thought. I can't say anything yet.

"I've moved into your room . . . While your father's away. It was always the sunniest room and now you'll not be needing it. Besides, it's not as big, not as empty . . . "

"Oh, Mummy!" Tracy said, a new softness in her voice, and her eyes sought Ross's. "We won't be long."

Throughout the meal the newlyweds talked nonstop about all the places they'd seen.

"Where has Dad taken off to?" Tracy asked, sitting back replete. "Mmm! That was good. The best meal we've had, wasn't it, Ross. No, don't answer that."

Ross didn't and the silence lengthened. Now she had to say something, tell them.

Margaret stood up, moving to fiddle with the ornaments by the fireplace.

"Your father's gone."

"Yes, you said . . . but . . . He often goes away on business."

"But this isn't business. This time he's not coming back." Margaret walked to the window, staring out over the garden, unable to meet their eyes.

"He's left me.

"Of course, I wouldn't want him back." She spoke calmly, though her fingers twisted together, whitening with the pressure she put on them. "It was his decision. There's a woman . . . "

Suddenly she faced them, the words tumbling out, bitter and angry.

"He never consulted me, never thought how I'd feel. There'll be money, he said. You won't want for anything, he said. Well, good rid . . . " Her voice faltered and, with horror she watched something dawn in Tracy's eyes before they switched quickly to Ross. Margaret took a couple of steps towards them.

It wasn't realisation she had read in those brief seconds when her daughter's guard was down, but knowledge, confirmation of something.

"You knew?" The words were

94

whispered, a question which carried an accusation. "You knew, and you didn't say."

"Mother!" Tracy jumped to her feet. "It wasn't like that. I didn't know anything . . . not really." She looked to Ross for help, but he simply shrugged, though he got up to come and stand beside her.

"I saw him once . . . with someone," Tracy admitted miserably.

Questions trembled on Margaret's lips but she didn't ask them. Instead she turned to the sideboard, pouring a drink, gesturing to the other two to help themselves. Was this why her daughter's greeting had been a little warmer? The glass between her hands she sat down again, staring into the liquid.

"Well, it doesn't matter now," she said, brushing aside Tracy's mumbled excuses and apologies. "I've told you; it's finished as far as I'm concerned. Over, done with. I'll make my own life from here on."

Tracy cursed angrily under her breath.

"He always was a selfish beggar."

Margaret's head shot up. She hadn't known Tracy realised that. Yes, Keith had always been selfish. Perhaps that, too was her fault, she should have broken the habits ingrained by his mother.

"What will you do?"

"Find a job, I suppose. I did a lot of your father's paperwork. He'll miss me for that," Margaret smiled, gloatingly.

Tracy ignored the look. "Mother, you've not worked for years. Anyway, why should you? If Dad said . . . and you . . . you've always been here."

Margaret grimaced. "I have, haven't I? Do you know, that was one of the things your father said? That I was a mother and nothing else? Well, I aim to change all that. Do my own thing."

She recalled the meeting and what she had said to that other woman. Had she been giving herself advice? It certainly fitted.

"Do my own thing. Isn't that what you young people say, these days? Well, now it's my turn."

She watched Tracy and Ross exchange glances once more, but this time she fancied there was a tinge of admiration in the look they shared.

★ ★ ★

Over the next few weeks Margaret applied for several jobs. On the morning of her first interview she woke up feeling almost confident, — until she saw the time. She stared at the clock, shaking it peevishly. She'd overslept. She had set the alarm, it hadn't rung.

"Damn you!" She slammed the instrument down. "I'll never be there on time now. How can I hope to get work?"

Running through to the kitchen she switched on the kettle then darted back to the wardrobe, pulling out a skirt and blouse and stepping into them, pushing her feet into a pair of shoes. Giving a cursory glance in the mirror she dashed back to the kitchen as the smell of burning toast rose to greet her.

Again, she swore, thinking she was growing more like her daughter every day. The toaster was new. It had been a tiny act of rebellion to buy it when Keith left. He wouldn't have 'unnecessary gadgets', as he called them, in the house, he'd always declared. Now, Margaret wondered what his live-in girl friend thought of that quirk.

"First the clock and now you," she snarled, dropping the offending burnt offering into the waste bin. "You've never been right since I bought you. You and your micro-chip! I ought to take you back. Keith always did say I was hopeless with anything mechanical."

Keith! He had always dealt with anything like this. He'd been the one to complain, to order repair men.

"Well, there's no one here to do it now," she told Barney. "But I can't let that — that thing, defeat me. What did I say to Tracy, the other night?"

Slowly, Margaret pushed the toaster back into its box.

★ ★ ★

The large, electrical goods department was busy when she walked up to a counter. Margaret put the box and its contents down on the glass display case. A young man behind it paused in his conversation with a fellow assistant.

"There's a cash point over there, Madam."

"I don't want to pay anything."

The man turned, slowly, a look on his face which spoke of the trials and tribulations of his job.

"I'm sorry. I don't understand."

"Neither do I. I don't understand why you sell things which don't work," Margaret said, bitingly.

"Our merchandise is of the highest quality. Perhaps you didn't understand the directions, Madam. Shall

I demonstrate? These micro-chips, so new, so clever . . . "

Margaret held on to her temper. "That toaster doesn't toast bread, it incinerates it; or it doesn't switch on at all. I want my money back."

"If it is faulty, — " Clearly the man didn't believe it was, "we'd be pleased to exchange it," he said, beginning to unpack the toaster.

"I've just told you it's faulty. And I do not want another. I want my money back. I believe I am entitled to that. I did bring the toast." Margaret reached into her bag with a wicked smile.

"Er . . . that won't be necessary, I'm sure we can take your word for it. But wouldn't you like to choose another toaster? A different make, if this isn't to your liking?"

Margaret raised her voice, ever so slightly. She'd had enough of this.

"I like my toast lightly done, nicely golden. Your toaster burned the bread."

Heads were turning and the man was beginning to look uncomfortable.

100

"I'll . . . I'll arrange a refund. If you'd just come this way."

Margaret nodded, smiling at him and at those customers who hovered nearby. Then she followed the man towards the pay desk. As he counted the money into her hand Margaret experienced a heady feeling of triumph. She'd done it! She'd actually done it!

The feeling lasted all the way from town and, on turning towards the avenue she knew she could keep it to herself no longer. Casting a swift glance into the driving mirror she swung the car in a sharp turn and came to a halt in the next street.

Elizabeth Short opened the door to her and, though she looked faintly surprised, she led her visitor through to the sitting-room with a welcoming smile.

"Coffee?" she asked.

"Mmm! And toast. No, I don't really mean that," Margaret laughed. "Just coffee will be fine."

"I expect I could rustle up a

biscuit." Elizabeth eyed Margaret. "What's happened? Of course! You got the job!"

"Job? Oh, no! Truth is I was late and then I forgot to go." Margaret's eyes gleamed.

Since that first encounter with this woman at the committee meeting, the two of them had chatted casually whenever they chanced to meet, but Margaret had somehow known that this was the one person who would understand now.

"*If you'd ever like to talk*," Elizabeth had said, that day Margaret had turned the chairman from her house. "*I'll be around.*"

Perhaps this wasn't quite what she had had in mind, Margaret thought now, but she was sure the other woman would understand.

"Forgot? You forgot? Then, Margaret, where ever have you been? If I didn't know you, I'd say you were drunk. Come on! Out with it!"

"I think perhaps I am a little drunk.

I took back my toaster.

"I told you it didn't work. Well, I finally took it back to the shop. *And*, I got my money back."

"Maybe you should have that drink," Elizabeth grinned. "But, on the other hand, maybe coffee will sober you up."

"Lovely," Margaret agreed, flicking her hair back as she caught sight of herself in a mirror.

She paused, examining the woman who looked back at her. There was something different; something about the way she stood, held her head, a look in her eyes. She's a woman who can cope. The thought came to Margaret before she had fully realised she was looking at her own reflection.

She turned quickly. "Elizabeth, remember talking the other day? About clothes and things?

"Well, will you come shopping with me?"

"Yes, certainly, if that's what you want . . . but, why?"

"Because you always look so . . . "
Margaret sketched vaguely in the air.
"So right. And also," she laughed, a
little sheepishly. "I've discovered that
underneath the layers of fat that, praise
be, I seem to have been shedding quite
rapidly, lately, there's a whole new
me wanting to get out. So, will you
help?"

Elizabeth smiled. "Haven't I always
dreamed of spending someone else's
money? Of course I'll come. It should
be fun."

5

MARGARET'S spirits were still high as she let herself into Brook House sometime later and she called loudly for Barney, needing someone to share her feeling of well being. But there was no sign of the little dog.

"Hey! Where are you, Barney? Come on, love. You're not sulking, are you, because I was a bit longer than I said. Okay! So I'm sorry, boy," she chuckled, going through to the kitchen.

Barney was curled in his basket and though he raised his head as she entered there was no welcoming thump of his tail.

"Barney? Barney, love? Are you still sick? Oh, Barney!"

Lifting him into her arms Margaret perched on a stool, her fingers running over him caressingly, touching his muzzle gently. He tried to lick her fingers, but the move was half-hearted and he whimpered as she touched him.

"I think it's the vet for you, my lad," she said, trying to make her voice light. She glanced towards his empty water bowl which she'd filled before she left the house earlier. "It looks as if you've got a temperature. Never mind. We'll soon have you feeling better."

The waiting-room at the vets' surgery was quite full, and Margaret was reminded of her visit to the doctors as she looked round the newly appointed rooms.

Barney had been Keith's dog, originally bought with the children in mind, but he had soon adopted Margaret, once he discovered who fed and exercised him. Yet Keith had brought him here, on the odd occasions he'd needed attention.

"It's much nicer now, isn't it?" A voice broke into her thoughts. "My

Rosie doesn't mind coming so much now."

Margaret turned to find an elderly woman smiling at her, a cat curled on her knees.

"I haven't been for ages. Luckily Barney's been very fit," she said, her voice a little strained as she touched the dog's ears, comfortingly. "But he's pretty sick, now, I'm afraid. Must be. I don't think he even noticed your cat."

"Mmm! He does look quiet, poor thing. But Rosie's used to dogs. I've got a terrier myself. They get along fine, at least, they do when Rosie's well." She sighed. "The vet says it's nothing much. Gave me some pills for her, but danged if I can get her to swallow them. I've tried everything I can think of. Crushed them in milk, hidden them in fish."

Despite her anxiety the woman slapped her knees and chuckled.

"But, she's a caution, is Rosie. Just looks at her dish and then up at me as if to say, 'who do you think you're kidding'. I even gave her some tinned salmon the other day. Now, wouldn't you have thought she'd eat that up without any trouble? But, would she? You'd have thought it was bad the way she turned up her nose. I tell you, I'm at my wits end. That's why we're here again, isn't it, Rosie?"

She stroked the cat's fur and Margaret watched a moment. Then she spoke, hesitantly at first but gathering courage as she went on.

"They can be difficult, I know. We had a cat once. But, there is a knack to it. Er . . . have you got one of the pills? Perhaps I could show you. It's quite simple, when you know how."

"Would you? Oh, that is kind. Then I wouldn't have to bother the vet. I don't like Rosie being off colour. She's a real friend, is Rosie, company, you know."

Margaret nodded, remembering how much closer she'd grown to Barney these past weeks; how much he'd helped her. Instinctively, her hand tightened round him. He must get well. He must!

"Here it is. Rosie won't scratch, or nothing. That's, if you don't mind."

The doubt in the older woman's voice finally reached Margaret and she summoned a smile, banishing her fears for Barney.

"Of course I don't. There's nothing to worry about. See!"

Margaret slipped her hands under the cat and deftly turned her on her back.

"Now hold still," she told her. "That's it. Catch hold of her front paws, please. It's all right, Rosie. No one's going to hurt you," she assured the cat as it opened its mouth in a plaintive miaow.

"There!" Quickly she popped the pill into the tiny pink mouth. "Now, we rub her throat, like this, and . . . There! Did you see her swallow? It's gone now."

"And so will my livelihood, young woman," A voice said above the two women's bent heads.

Margaret jerked upright, colour rushing into her face.

"If you keep doing my job for me," the man went on sternly, but his words were belied by the twinkle in his eyes and the upward tilt of his lips.

"You're not a vet, are you?" he asked, then answered his own question. "No, of course not, or you wouldn't be here with that little chap. You certainly have a way with animals. I know from past experience that Rosie's no push-over, is she Mrs Blake?"

"She's certainly not, Mr Andrews. You did say those tablets were all she needed, didn't you?"

The man nodded, and Mrs Blake got to her feet. "Then I'll not be needing to trouble you any further. My friend here showed me how to get them down Rosie. Come on, you little minx, you. Wasting Mr Andrew's time, and mine. It's home for you and no more nonsense in future. Do you know, I think, sometimes, it's the bus ride down here, she likes, that I do."

Mrs Blake pushed her pet, none too gently, into the basket she brought from beneath the chair, and Margaret watched in dismay.

"I'll say goodbye, then. And thanks, thanks very much." She nodded towards Margaret. "Good day to you, Mr Andrews."

Margaret mumbled a reply, keeping her eyes fastened on the plump figure as she made for the door. But as it closed behind her she was forced to meet the vet's gaze.

"I, I'm sorry. I didn't . . ."

"That's all right, my dear." Again the faded eyes behind the gold rimmed spectacles smiled at her. "I wouldn't have charged Mrs Blake, anyway. She's an old and valued customer. And having said that, I have to admit, that in all the years she's been seeking my advice, I've never thought to give her that particular little piece. Somehow, one expects people to know," he smiled, shrugging his shoulders. "Very remiss of me."

He turned away. "Rusty, next, is it? Bring him in, will you?" he told the dog's owner.

He was gone with scarcely a nod in Margaret's direction and she was left to wonder just how much, or how little, she had offended him. He had smiled, but that might have been mere politeness.

If Barney hadn't been so obviously sick, she might very well have got up and gone home. As it was, the minutes dragged until she was the last person in the waiting room when Mr Andrews looked round the door and beckoned her inside.

The modernisation of the premises hadn't extended too far into Mr Andrew's consulting room, though the examination table gleamed with chrome and tiles and the instruments shone from equally bright trays, the comfortable leather chair beside the desk spoke of years of use.

"Ah! The contestant for my title," he teased, indicating she should lie Barney on the table, as he moved towards the sink. Over the sound of running water he questioned Margaret, nodding at her answers but making no comment. Coming back to the table he showed that he wished her to go on holding the dog.

"I used to have an assistant; a nice young woman. Perhaps a bit too nice. Some fellow snapped her up. Now she's got other things than animals, at least the four legged kind, to take care of. Matthew — Matthew Sayers that is, my partner, keeps urging me to engage someone else, but . . . I don't know."

He looked up from the notes he was making, studying Margaret over the pinnacle of his fingers.

"We manage. Most owners don't mind holding their pets, unless it gets awkward, distressing, you understand. Then, there's generally the other one of us." His eyes went to the connecting door. "Matthew says I'm too particular, but . . . you can have all the book learning you want, it doesn't necessarily follow that you're in sympathy with the animals."

"I suppose not."

"Everyone doesn't have the instinctive understanding you seem to have, my dear. That's only given to a chosen few."

Margaret hid her blushes under cover of putting Barney's medicine into her handbag.

"I, I do like animals, always have. I used to think . . . " she began in a rush, then stopped, getting to her feet. "But . . . Thank you."

"Thank you. What did you used to think?" Mr Andrews pressed.

"Oh! Oh, just that I'd like to have worked with animals, been a kennel-maid, or something. But in my young days they didn't get paid much," she smiled.

"I doubt they fare much better now."

The vet came round the front of his desk. "Perhaps Matthew's right," he said, thoughtfully. "Perhaps I shouldn't go on expecting miracles. And we do need some help around here. Ah, well!" He extended his hand. "Goodbye, Mrs Draycott. Goodbye."

They walked towards the door. "If you should ever want anything to do . . . find yourself at a loose end, that . . . but no. You're busy, of course. It was just . . . you seem to fit the bill, but I expect you are busy. Goodbye, again."

"But, I'm not." Margaret swung round. "Not busy, I mean. I've nothing to do. Not enough, anyway. You see . . . Oh! What I'm trying to say is that I'd be glad to help out. I'm not qualified but I could hold the animals, that sort of thing."

Once again she felt herself blushing and she groped for the door. "Yes, well, goodbye. And . . . "

"But I just got through telling you I don't want someone qualified? There's Matthew and myself, we don't need help in that sphere. Do you mean it,

Mrs Draycott? Would you be willing to act as, as doorkeeper, nurse, pill dispenser," he grinned, "and general dogsbody, around here? On a proper basis, of course?"

"I . . . I was simply offering to help out. I thought, until you got someone else."

"I don't want someone else. I'm offering you the job. I think you'd do very well, and if, as you say, you have no other commitments . . . "

There was a sharp rap on the communicating door and it opened as Margaret and Mr Andrews turned towards it.

The man who stood in the opening smiled apologetically at Margaret, then spoke to the vet.

"Sorry, John. I thought you were free. I'll come back later."

"No, Matthew. There's no need to do that. We are almost finished. Anyway, I'd like to introduce Mrs Draycott. She's got quite a way with animals, Matthew."

The younger man smiled, nodding to Margaret but the smile was mere politeness and his gaze returned to his partner.

"Matthew, Mrs Draycott — Margaret," he amended, glancing at Barney's card, "has offered to work for us. We haven't discussed details, of course; I was waiting to speak to you; but I'm sure she'll fit in here just fine."

He faced Margaret, apparently unaware of the startled, irritated expression on Matthew Sayers's face.

"I have your phone number, haven't I? We'll be in touch, Margaret. We must arrange a time when you can come in and fix everything up."

"Yes. Er . . . yes. Thanks! Er, goodbye, Mr Sayers." Margaret kept her eyes fixed on the younger of the two men. Tall, dark haired, as Mr Andrews had evidently once been, with the same blue eyes and clean cut features, he could easily have been the older man's son.

But, she realised, meeting Matthew

Sayers's unflinching gaze, there the resemblance ended. There seemed little of the milk of human kindness in this man's face. No sparkle in his eyes, no laughter wrinkles round his eyes and the set of his shoulders spoke of an unbending disposition.

"Goodbye," she said quietly, including the two men in her slight smile, and closed the door behind her.

Her fingers had scarcely left the door knob, her feet moved a step, before Matthew Sayers's voice came to her.

"John! Have you gone mad? This is crazy. I know we need someone, but we don't even know that woman. She hasn't any training, I gather. And no experience either. What's the point of hiring someone who'll probably be more of a liability?"

She didn't wait to hear any more, gathering Barney closer to her breast she hurried out to the car.

What did it matter what that odious man said? She wouldn't take the job now, even if it was offered to her.

And it won't be, she thought, putting Barney on to the seat beside her. Mr Andrews won't telephone. Of course he won't.

However, a few days later, there was a call, and despite Margaret's misgivings she found herself agreeing to come into the surgery three days a week, oftener if the need arose.

"You'll be kept busy," John had told her. "We've had no secretarial help for some time, never mind anything else. Matthew's glad you're able to help out there."

If he isn't happy about anything else, Margaret thought. Okay! I'll not expect him to ask for my help in any other capacity. It's no skin off my nose. I'll be working, that's all I care about.

She had told John a little of her story, saying she was alone now, allowing him to make his own deductions. She didn't want sympathy, and especially not from Matthew Sayers.

It was soon clear she wasn't going to get any. Mr Sayers was always polite and there the association ended.

She was working busily when Matthew Sayers came into the waiting-room one morning.

Hearing the door open she looked up, a smile on her face, expecting to see John.

"Oh, good morning, Mr Sayers. Er . . . John, Mr Andrews, rang in. He's gone straight over to Mile End farm."

The younger vet nodded. "Thanks!" Then, noting the littered desk, he hesitated.

"What are you doing? Lost something?" He barked.

"No. No, of course not! It's just that the other day; Mr Andrews was asking about something; I noticed there are a lot of treatments which come up regularly, — injections and things. I thought it might help if I marked those files and cross-referenced them. I, there's nothing else waiting."

"O . . oh!"

The single syllable was drawn out as Matthew Sayers continued to stare at a point an inch or two above Margaret's head, and Margaret's jaw tightened.

"You've no objections, have you?" she asked, when the man didn't speak.

"No." He turned to face her. "I did understand that there was such a record kept, even before you came."

Margaret swallowed, holding on to her temper.

Why couldn't this man accept that she had been useful during the weeks she'd worked here, despite her lack of qualifications? Why was he always so stand-offish?

The first day John Andrews had told her to drop the mister, when there were no clients around, and he'd called her Margaret from the first. But the younger partner had never relaxed, never addressed her in any other than a completely formal manner. And now, the implication that she was wasting her or probably he thought, their, time, since they were paying her, — made her see red.

"No doubt you're right, Sir." The

last word was fringed with ice. "But I believe it is some time since you had anyone on a regular basis. Whatever records were supposed to be kept haven't been updated. However, if there is something of a more pressing nature?"

She left the question hanging between them, her eyes going tellingly round the empty waiting-room.

Matthew Sayers, she noted, had the grace to look uncomfortable, but his brow gathered with anger too.

"Did Mr Andrews say when he thought he would get back?" he asked, coldly.

"The only message I've received is the one I gave you, Mr Sayers. There have been no other calls."

Margaret picked up a filing card and sat, fingers poised to put it into place, and after a moment, Matthew coughed, lowering his head and muttering a short thank you, through the hand he raised to cover his mouth.

She waited until the door closed

behind him before giving vent to her anger. Then throwing the card down, she swore.

Of all the unmitigated, boorish men, Matthew Sayers was the worst.

Thank goodness he's so against employing a mere female, and one without qualifications, that he scarcely admits to my presence, and seldom asks for my help.

If it wasn't that I'm enjoying working, especially here, I'd give in my notice. I couldn't let John down now. If only there wasn't that one fly in the ointment, she thought, picking up the card once more. She couldn't help smiling as she viewed the card with its list of drugs which had been administered. Her simile had been very apt, ointments played a large part in her work. Not to mention flies, she decided, a moment later, coming across a reference to warble flies.

Her humour increased when the word caught her attention again. Apparently there was more than one sort of warble. Horses could have warbles of another kind.

She read on, her interest increasing. This warble was a swelling on a horse's back, caused by the rubbing of its saddle.

"The poor thing! Redwood Stables! I reckon you ought to take better care of your animals, Mr Owner."

The stables was no twopenny-halfpenny affair, either, she noted, going on to read about the stud horses and brood mares.

"Huh! There must be a tidy bit of money salted away in all that lot. Proprietor. L. Jennings," she mused.

Jennings? Jennings? Now, where had she heard that name?

Margaret swallowed, finding difficulty in breathing as her heart pounded.

There had been a time, not so very long ago, when she had heard the name often, she realised. And the memories it stirred now weren't ones she wanted dragged up.

Keith had used the name, frequently.

Derisively, angrily and often with frank envy. If there had been others present he had modified his tone, a little, sounding almost pleasant as he spoke of some meeting with the director of his firm, hinting that the two of them were on close terms.

But that man was called Roy Jennings. Good old Roy, sometimes, Margaret recalled with anguish. She had thought she was managing to forget Keith, had battened down that compartment of her memory. But now she realised she would never fully be able to do that. Not until she could eradicate every trace of him from her life. And how could she ever do that?

6

WHEN the telephone rang, later that morning Margaret lifted the receiver, her attention still on the clients' cards before her.

"Good morning! Andrews and Sayers, Veterinaries. Can I help you?"

"Mm!" The girl's voice was hesitant, but it only took Margaret a moment to recognise it.

"Tracy! However did you get this number? I'd sooner you didn't ring me here," she said, casting a glance over her shoulder to Matthew Sayers's room.

"Mother! How can I help it? You're never in at home, at least, I've never managed to get hold of you. Ian told me where you were working. Good for you, Mum. You said you'd find a job. How are you liking it?"

"Fine! Very much! Tracy, was there

something special you wanted?"

"Yes. But do I have to have a reason to talk to my mother?"

Margaret spoke shortly. "You always had; — as I remember it."

"Oh! Well! Well, I want to talk to you now. I thought maybe I could see you?"

"You mean come up home? But you've not long since gone back. I thought you were supposed to be studying. You'll never get your degree this way."

"I, I thought . . . Just a flying visit. Just to . . . say hello and . . . talk."

"Tracy, I warn you, if this is leading up to asking, to come back home, well, you've made your bed . . . "

"And I must lie in it. Yes, Mother, I know. It's nothing like that. We're fine! But, I would like to see you. Just for an hour or two."

"Aren't you well?"

"Mother! What is all this? I said I wanted to see you, have a chat. It's no big deal."

Margaret felt on the defensive and the feeling made her angry.

"Tracy, I do know you. There's something else. If you aren't sick . . . "

"No, Mother. I told you, I'm great! Look, I know we haven't always seen eye to eye but it's different now. I'm married and . . . Well, it is different, isn't it?"

"I suppose so." Margaret shook her head in bewilderment. Could this really be Tracy talking? The child who had never wanted any help or, apparently, affection from the day she could walk unaided.

"You are sure there's nothing wrong? I couldn't stand you telling me your troubles, I've got enough of my own. And wives never do understand their husband. I never understood your father," she added, bitterly.

"Mum, I'm sorry about Dad and what's happened. But I keep telling you I'm not in any trouble."

"Okay then. When were you thinking of coming?"

"Well, I'm here, at home, actually. That's where I'm ringing from. Not knowing about the job, naturally, I thought you'd be here. You always were. Mum?" Tracy spoke again before Margaret could make any comment on that last remark. "Where's Barney?"

"Things have changed, Tracy." The words answered the accusation in Tracy's voice when she'd spoken of those times when she'd come in from school to find her mother waiting.

Not that she'd ever seemed to notice my presence, Margaret thought ruefully.

"I have to leave Barney with a friend; — Liz Short, you don't know her. He can't be alone all day."

"Oh! I thought you'd be back for lunch. I have to go home tonight."

Margaret glanced towards her shopping bag with its flask of coffee and container of salad.

"I could meet you, I suppose. What about the Red Lion? We could eat there. You know where it is?"

129

"Yes." Tracy sounded amused. "I'm just surprised that you do."

"I go there sometimes."

A door clicked and Margaret sensed Matthew Sayers watching her.

"I must go now, Tracy. Twelve thirty, okay?"

She didn't hear Tracy's reply, putting the receiver down quickly.

"Did you want something, Mr Sayers?"

"Just a file. But don't trouble yourself. I'm sure I can find it."

The vet crossed behind her chair to the filing cabinets and Margaret waited until she had the outer room to herself, once more, before giving vent to her feelings.

Of course it had had to be *him*. Why couldn't Tracy, have phoned when John was in? He'd never have been so coolly polite, so, so . . . insufferable!

Why had Tracy phoned anyway? Okay, she'd come up, and it would have been stupid to go back to Birmingham without seeing her mother. But why had she come? Why? And so soon after she and Ross had paid a visit?

The Red Lion was already quite full when Margaret entered and she wandered around, glancing into the different areas before noticing Tracy sitting in a corner, alone. Her daughter lifted a hand as their eyes met, and Margaret smiled a greeting.

As she threaded her way towards Tracy the smile vanished, leaving her feeling slightly irritated. Tracy looked decidedly unkempt.

It wasn't simply the sloppy clothes her generation often adopted, it went deeper than that. Of course she had travelled up from Birmingham, and trains could be grubby, but she had been to the house. Why hadn't she washed, and brushed her hair?

Margaret's fingers went instinctively to the crisp collar of the blouse she was wearing, conscious that the soft pink suited her colouring and that the pencil slim skirt fitted perfectly. She had also checked her hair and make-up before leaving the car. Couldn't Tracy have made some attempt?

"Hi!" Margaret brought back the smile as she slid into the seat alongside her daughter. "Have you ordered?"

"No, I thought I'd wait. I got a drink though."

Margaret eyed the glass. "It's only juice," Tracy supplied and Margaret bit her lip.

She hadn't meant to start off on the wrong foot, and anyway, why shouldn't Tracy have a drink? She wasn't a child.

She picked up the menu. "I think I'll have a salad. What about you?"

"The same. Ham, I think." Tracy's eyebrows lifted as her mother asked for cottage cheese.

"Mum! You have lost weight, or rather, you've not put it back after . . ."

"No. I'm glad to say I haven't. There was a time when I found it impossible to slim." Margaret laughed, shortly. "Your father did me one good turn, it seems."

Tracy's fingers moved, but they stopped short of actually touching her mother's hand.

"It suits you. Being slim, I mean. You look quite different."

A smile touched Margaret's lips. Why couldn't anyone in her family bring themselves to say she looked smart, or sophisticated, or maybe even chic? Clearly such words didn't apply to 'good old Mum'.

Ian and Janet were just the same. Janet had even hinted there might be something wrong, and asked if she was 'looking after herself properly'. None of her children seemed to want to acknowledge that the *hausfrau* they had known didn't exist any more. Her tone was a little sharp when she asked Tracy, again, what it was she'd come to talk about.

"It surely wasn't my figure. Though," she glanced over at Tracy, "seems to me you could do with watching what you eat, Tracy. Shouldn't you be learning from my mistakes?"

133

"Oh, Mum! It wasn't only . . . " The girl blushed. "I didn't mean . . . I'm sorry."

"You mean, your father didn't leave me simply because I'd . . . what's the popular phrase . . . let myself go? Hm! I'd already worked that out for myself."

"Mummy!"

Margaret blinked and eyed her daughter keenly. Mummy? Tracy hadn't used that word since she was a toddler.

There was something . . . something about her eyes. Something . . . ? And she had put on weight, it wasn't only that ghastly skirt and tee-shirt she was wearing.

"Mum . . . I'm pregnant."

Margaret felt a prick of triumph. She'd almost got there without telling. But her pleasure was short lived. When Ian and Tracy had begun to leave babyhood way behind, and she'd begun to see that, one day, they wouldn't need her, she had started to dream of the time when she would be a granny. It would be lovely. All the fun with none of the hard work. She'd have her babies back again, be needed. Now, Tracy's news only made her conscious of her age. She struggled to make the right responses.

"Are you keeping well? Looking after yourself? You've someone else to consider now, you know."

"Mother! I thought you'd be pleased? Aren't you?"

"Are you? Do you and Ross want this baby? And so soon? You don't seem very sure."

"Of course! Well, Ross does. But he's not got to have it. I thought I was happy, too, at first. Well, it's all right then, isn't it? But . . . Look at me! And this is only the beginning. I shan't be able to go anywhere, do anything, even after it's born. Not for ages, anyway. Huh! It's all right for Ross."

"It usually is, for the fathers. Having the baby is generally considered to be some consolation for the mothers. It was to me."

"You've changed," Tracy accused her.

"That's true, I have," Margaret agreed, after a moment's consideration. "Because I had to. When circumstances alter you've got to go with them, or sink. Tracy, you must have wanted this baby. Your generation does have more of a choice in these matters than we had. I didn't choose what happened to me, either when you were born, or when your father left me."

"Don't keep saying *your father*. Hasn't Dad got a name any longer?" Tracy cried. Then she flushed, avoiding her mother's eyes. "I'm sorry! It's just Dad not being here and, and I thought you'd have been happy about the baby."

"I am happy. Babies are nice to have around. They're sweet and cuddly, and can bring a lot of happiness and fun. But, this is your baby, Tracy. No doubt I shall coo over it when it's born, like any other besotted granny, but . . . "

She hesitated. How could she tell Tracy that she felt afraid to give her love, afraid of getting it tossed back at her, afraid to be hurt again.

She laid down her knife and fork, carefully, across her empty plate.

"Let's wait and see, my dear. And, as for the blues you're feeling at the moment, it's par for the course." She wiped her mouth and picked up the bill.

"You'll be fine. Eat sensibly; get enough rest without lolling about; and you'll get through without any problems, like we all do."

She glanced at her watch. "It's getting late."

"Mum!" Tracy put out a hand, catching at her mother's sleeve. "I thought you'd . . . Well, you haven't said a word about college, or asked whether we can afford a baby, or anything."

Margaret smiled wryly. Tracy was right, she had changed. Once these would have been her first questions. Now, she didn't seem to care. She had stopped living her children's lives, stopped living through them.

"Tracy, I didn't want you to get married so young, in the first place, if you remember. But you would have your way. Oh! Of course! That was why." Realisation sprang to her eyes. "I suppose I should have guessed. Perhaps I did, but, what with everything else . . . Anyway, you reminded me, then that it was your life." She got to her feet.

"We all only have one life. Three months ago, mine changed, drastically it seemed at the time, though, on reflection, maybe it wasn't as catastrophic as . . .

"Look, I've got to get back to the surgery. I'm late already." She put her hands on her daughter's shoulders, moving them slowly to frame her face as the girl looked up at her. Then she kissed Tracy's cheek.

"Take care of yourself, my dear. Look after that grandchild of mine."

"But . . . Mother! Mum! I . . . I'll keep in touch," she added, as Margaret backed away.

Reaching the exit Margaret turned to wave, smiling and nodding as Tracy waved excitedly back. Then, swinging abruptly round she almost cannoned into a man who had just come through the door and was gazing around him.

"Sorry," Margaret smiled up into his face as he stepped aside. But the smile faded.

She would never know whether she actually said his name, but if she did her husband didn't hear her. His eyes slid over her, their expression vague, his smile polite, as he waved to someone across the room, before, with a slight incline of his head strode away.

Somehow Margaret managed to get out into the street, disbelief and anger warring inside her.

Keith had ignored her! He'd looked right through her as if she was a total stranger. Tears of frustration and pity welled in her eyes and she turned towards the row of shop windows, staring unseeingly at the goods displayed, in an effort to conceal her misery.

But as she pretended to examine the dresses she saw someone watching her. A woman, looking into the window also. A smart, slim, woman whose dark hair was a shining cap around her slightly elfin features. A poised, confident woman; except that there was something about her eyes? A kind of mistiness, almost as if she was crying! Margaret swung her head sideways and the woman turned also, and Margaret began to laugh. She'd been gazing at her own reflection. No wonder Keith had walked past her. He hadn't recognised her.

"My!" She breathed. "What a turn up for the books. Just wait until I tell

Liz. She'll really appreciate this one."

With a renewed spring in her step she turned to where she'd parked her car, and it was only when she was seated behind the wheel that she remembered John Andrews's request that she would deliver a package of drugs to Matthew Sayers's home.

Now she glanced towards the dashboard where she had locked the small parcel. Perhaps he won't be in, she thought. John had said Matthew would collect the drugs later. I can only hope, she grinned, turning the car towards the outskirts of the town.

Twenty-seven, Broughton Gardens, was a more imposing house than Margaret had expected. In fact, she'd thought Matthew Sayers probably lived in a service flat.

She rang the bell, a little timidly, pinning a bright, non-committal smile on her face.

After a while the door was opened by a girl of about sixteen; all bright blue hair and eye make-up.

Margaret swallowed her curiosity.

"Could I speak to Mr Sayers, please?"

The girl shook her head. "Sorry! Dad's out."

"Oh!" Margaret was as much dumbfounded by the information that Matthew Sayers had a daughter, as by the daughter herself. "Er . . . I've got something for him. I work at the surgery," she explained. "Mr Andrews asked me to call. Perhaps I could speak to Mrs Sayers?"

"There isn't . . . There's only Dad and me."

It was a statement of fact, given without any sign of emotion, but its very bareness told Margaret so much.

"Oh!" she murmured, her voice loosing its brisk note. And the girl reacted with something close to antagonism.

Pulling the door wider, she said, brightly. "Come in and wait, why don't you? But I'm not sure if he'll be back, until this evening."

142

"Er . . . that's kind of you. But I understood your father does mean to call in for these." She held out the package.

"Then leave the stuff with me. I won't eat them, you know," she added, smiling maliciously.

A hand, lifting involuntarily to her spiky hair, spoke of defiance, and Margaret wondered about this girl and Matthew Sayers. He so correct, so . . . stuffy. She so modern. How did they get along? What sort of companionship could they share? He in his sober business suits and she glowing with colour.

Margaret pulled up her thoughts, conscious that the girl was eyeing her.

She grinned back. "I never imagined you would. They probably taste awful, anyway. But, you will see he gets them? You're not going out, or anything? I wouldn't want him to think I forgot to deliver the drugs."

"Don't worry! It'll be all right. Dad give you a rough time, does he? Don't

143

let it bother you. He's an old softie, really."

"John said . . . " Margaret broke off. It certainly wasn't the place to reveal that John Andrews had implied something similar. "John said the tablets were urgent," she amended.

"That's okay! I will see he gets them the minute he comes in. See you!"

Margaret walked back to her car.

An old softie? Soft was the last adjective she would have applied to Matthew Sayers. Neither was he old. Maybe a year or two older than me, she mused. I wonder what happened to his wife? There isn't, the girl had begun, then changed her mind. Was the tragedy so recent that she couldn't bring herself to speak of her mother?

There's only Dad and me. The words had a pitiful ring, despite the girl's harsh exterior, reminding her of Tracy's attitude when she'd spoken of Margaret's refusal to call Keith by name.

144

Poor kid! And poor Matthew, too.

It must be worse to be left that way than how I was. At least I could be angry. I could try to believe I was better off without Keith.

Remembering the days when she had shut herself away, ignoring even Barney's frantic distress, Margaret vowed she would try to be a little more understanding where Matthew Sayers was concerned.

Though why she should worry, she didn't know. Why should the emptiness of her employer's life make her feel sad?

"I only work for the dratted man," she cried. "Haven't I enough worries of my own? John and that girl can say what they like, if he's soft then so's granite."

★ ★ ★

It seemed that both Margaret's children had some news they wished to give her. Ian turned up that evening, just when she'd settled before the TV.

She went to brew coffee, returning with two mugs and a biscuit tin.

"I think there's some in. But, no cake, I'm afraid. I don't bake much, these days."

Ian looked uncomfortable, evidently putting his own construction on her words, hastening to reassure her.

"It doesn't matter. I expect it is . . . different, now . . . Er, how are you liking your job?"

"I enjoy it. Ian, I don't bake because there's only me to eat any cake, and I don't want it. Or hadn't you noticed how I look?"

"Of course! You've slimmed and . . . Mum, you don't want to take it too far. Janet's always been slim, but you, you're different. And it's not as if you're . . . "

"Young?" Margaret finished the sentence for him. "I'm certainly not old, Ian. Though it took your father's leaving to make me see that."

She wondered whether she should

tell him of the incident earlier that day when Keith had walked past her, but decided against it. Ian, she had learned, didn't like talking about his father's desertion. Margaret fancied he would have liked to defend Keith, but wasn't sure on what grounds.

"Is Janet busy?" she asked. "Or couldn't you get a sitter?"

"We didn't want to waste a sitter," Ian said, candidly. "Anyway I wanted to talk to you without Janet being here."

"Secrets?"

"Of course not!"

"Mum," Ian leant forward. "I've got this chance of another job."

"A promotion?"

"Not really."

"A better school then? That would be similar to promotion, wouldn't it?"

"Please listen, Mother. Yes, perhaps the school is better, in a way, though not more prestigious, which is what you meant. It's a place for handicapped children. We'd live in, as most of the children do. Actually, some of them are adults."

You mean mentally handicapped?" Margaret asked, being careful of the tone she used.

"Yes."

"And this is what you want to do? The sort of work you feel you can do?"

"Yes . . . Well, I'd have to have some training, but I've been attending courses. I'll learn as I go along, I expect. Why I'm asking your opinion is because the school's down south, Plymouth way. We'd be moving right away from you."

"What does Janet say to that? Does she mind leaving your home here?"

"No, I don't think so, not much, anyway. But I can't make up my mind. Should I go? Should I take this step, Mother?"

"It's your life, Ian."

"I know. But . . . It is a big step."

"Look! What do you want me to say? Do you want me to say what I think,

148

or simply back up what you've already decided?

"Because I think you should take this opportunity," she went on, when Ian shook his head in a helpless fashion. "Go! If that's what you want to do. Don't expect me to say stay, and then, in fifteen years or so, come back to me saying you should have done this. It's your life, Ian. You've got to make your own mistakes, and live with them, afterwards."

For several moments Ian sat, staring down at his clasped hands, and Margaret thought, he wanted me to tell him not to go. He was looking for a way out. Well, I won't be his scapegoat.

But, suddenly, Ian looked up and his face was alive with enthusiasm.

"Thanks, Mum! I thought you would say stay here. I was sure you'd want me to do the safe, steady thing, but I'm glad you don't."

He got to his feet. "It'll mean I won't be on hand, of course. But, it doesn't seem as if you're going to need me, not as I thought you would after Dad left. You've learned to cope."

There was a note of surprise in the words, and Margaret hid a smile.

Had he seen himself lumbered with his ageing mother? Perhaps it was that which had motivated this idea. Perhaps Janet had wanted him to cut the apron strings.

"Yes, I've learned a lot of things, Ian. And, somehow, I think I'm going to go on learning, I can't say I've forgotten, or forgiven, your father, but I'll never go to pieces the way I did, again. You can be sure of that. And I've learned something else," she added, thoughtfully. "When it comes down to brass tacks, we're all responsible for our own lives."

Impulsively, Ian took her hands, drawing her close. "You've nothing to blame yourself for, Mother."

"Maybe! But who can say?"

Ian put his arms round her, pressing his cheek against hers.

"Janet and Vicky will miss you, and so will I. I don't think I realised how much, until now," he said, smiling down into her face. "You're not such a bad old thing, are you?"

7

FEELING some sympathy for Matthew Sayers, and having her conscience prick her into deciding to be more tolerant of the younger vet, didn't make him any easier to work with. Margaret had to bite her tongue several times, over the next few days. The man doesn't want to be friendly, she decided. *He* doesn't try to understand me, or to make allowances for me being new here, so why should I consider him?

Thursdays, it had been decided between her and John, she could come in later if she wished, and this morning she had taken advantage of this to do some shopping. As the boot of her car wasn't very secure she had staggered into the waiting-room loaded with carrier bags. Of course, it had to be Matthew who was there, apparently waiting for her.

His eyes had gone to the clock, but he hadn't said anything. Which had given her no opportunity to remind him she wasn't exactly late, she thought, settling behind her desk. He'd simply given her a message.

"John's got Miss Jennings with him, so he won't want to be disturbed. And he took the Redwood file, just in case you miss it."

"Thanks for telling me. Will you be taking all the cases?"

Margaret glanced at the appointment book, reaching for the respective index cards.

"Of course! We can't send them away, can we? And John may have to go back with her to the stable. Yes, send them all into me, until you hear differently."

Margaret nodded, and when the vet had gone through into his own room she moved round the screen to where the clients were waiting.

"Mr Sayers will take surgery in a moment. We're sorry you've been kept waiting."

There were sympathetic nods all round and she went back to her desk, calling the first name when the light over Matthew's door glowed.

There was still no sign of John when, at last, the waiting-room was clear, and Margaret wondered what emergency was keeping the two enclosed in John's room so long. Obviously any of Miss Jennings's animals would have to be attended to back at the stables, but she knew that specimens were often brought in for testing from farms and other such places. Probably it was something on those lines now and the two were discussing the results.

It must be nice being one of the Miss Jennings of this world, with a rich father to finance one's dreams, she thought. Fancy owning a place like Redwood.

Could it possibly be the same Jennings? After all, Roy Jennings, the man Keith had spoken of, was a director of the firm Keith worked for.

The door of John's room opened some moments later and Margaret looked up, eager to see this favoured young woman. However, as she glanced past John, the womans face was hidden while she bent to search in her handbag.

"Margaret." John came towards her desk. "Matthew's coped, I expect? I see there's no one waiting."

"Yes, John, everything's under control. There weren't many people, anyway."

"Good! I hope there's not a lot this afternoon, either." He swung the appointment book to face him, running his finger down the entries. "No. I'll ask Matthew if he minds holding the fort again. I'm going out to Redwood."

"Oh! I hope there's nothing seriously wrong," Margaret said, looking to where the other woman was standing by the outer door, her back to them, politely studying the posters there while they talked.

"I don't think so, but we've got to get things cleared up. Oh! You haven't met Lydia, have you? Lydia . . ."

The woman turned, a polite smile on her lips and Margaret gave a little gasp as she looked into the woman's startling blue eyes.

"Lydia, this is Margaret. And what we've done without her help these last months, I can't imagine. Mrs Draycott walked in here one day with her dog and has scarcely left the place since. Have you, my dear?"

"No . . . er, no. I suppose not. I, I . . ." Margaret drew a deep breath. "How do you do, Miss Jennings."

She knew John was eyeing her, probably wondering whatever was making her behave this way, but she couldn't tell him. Couldn't even look at him. She seemed unable to take her eyes off the woman who was staring back at her, as if she, too, had seen a ghost.

But Margaret knew this was no ghost. Though Lydia Jennings hadn't seen her before she had obviously recognised the name. But Margaret knew this face. How could she ever forget it? It was the face which had loomed out of the darkness of Keith's car. The face of the woman who had driven the car which had taken her husband away from her.

Somehow, Margaret managed to smile, though there was no way she could have taken the other woman's hand, and, luckily, Lydia Jennings seemed to realise this. She nodded, smiling ever so slightly, and making no attempt to come nearer.

John Andrew watched her a moment, but then drew his own conclusions.

"Okay Lydia! Stop fretting! We're all set now. We can get on our way. See you, Margaret!"

"Yes! Bye! Bye!" Margaret murmured, lowering her head swiftly to the typewriter keyboard. When the door closed she shut her eyes tightly trying to blot out the scene. After a struggle, which seemed to last for hours, she managed to summon enough control to speak on the intercom to Matthew Sayers.

"I'm going for lunch, now, Mr Sayers; if there's nothing further?"

"No, no, that will be quite all right. I take it John's gone over to Redwood?"

Margaret sucked in air. "Yes."

"Oh! Oh, so that's under control. I . . . is there anything . . . Er, Mrs Draycott?"

"No, Mr Sayers. There are no messages."

She pressed the switch, closing the circuit, unable to trust herself to talk further, and frenziedly she gathered her bags and hurried from the office.

Having to walk through the crowded streets to the car park brought the necessary strength to hide the turmoil raging inside her. She even managed to start the car and drive out on to the main road, but there she felt the scalding tears begin to gather behind her eyes.

She had vowed that, never again, would she cry over Keith, but now, only the concentration necessary to steer through the traffic made it possible to stop the tears from falling.

Angrily, she dashed a hand across her eyes as the brake lights of the car in front blurred. Her foot jammed down on the brake pedal automatically, but her nerves jangled as the rear end of the other car rushed towards her.

For several seconds she sat, letting the honking traffic pass by; then she breathed, slowly and deeply, before switching on the engine once more.

Liz Short took one look at her friend's set, white face and put out her hands to pull Margaret inside.

"Come away in, my dear. The kettle's just on the boil."

Margaret allowed Liz to draw her through the hall into the cosy living-room, but when she opened her mouth, Liz pressed her fingers.

"Tea first, and, by the look of you,

something stronger might not go amiss; then we'll talk."

There was no need to tell Margaret to sit down, as Liz watched, her body folded and sank into a chair of its own volition.

When Liz came back, bearing two steaming mugs, Margaret didn't appear to have moved an inch. Pulling another chair close, Liz held out one mug.

"Drink!" she commanded, and dutifully, Margaret gulped the hot liquid.

She grimaced as she tasted the spirit Liz had added, but she was glad of the warmth it brought seeping back into her body.

"I've seen her," Margaret burst out. "The woman Keith went away with. I didn't recognise her, at first, but it's her, right enough. Those blue eyes. Didn't I tell you how bright blue they were? And long, blonde hair. Blonde! Someone made a film about blondes, once. *Gentlemen prefer blondes*, it was called. Well, I'll tell you one thing for nothing; Keith's no gentleman."

Liz made no attempt to halt the flow of words, her keen mind sifting through them to the core.

"He's a rat," Margaret went on. "Did you know that? My husband's . . . my one time husband . . . One time? Huh! That makes you think. I wonder how many others there have been?

"Oh, Liz!" Her voice cracked. "Liz! It was awful."

Margaret grabbed for the half-empty mug, swallowing the remaining liquid noisily.

"She's the boss's daughter. Keith's boss," she said, a little more steadily. "Can you believe that? Keith ran off with the Managing Director's daughter. Even in his unfaithfulness — " Her tongue slurred over the word. "Even then he was faithful to his beliefs. Look after number one, that was always Keith's code of ethics. Ethics! My God!"

"You met her? Today? How?"

"Didn't I tell you that? She came into the surgery, bold as brass. No, she wasn't like that. I don't suppose she was aware that I worked there. Give the woman her due, she was as startled as I was. When you think of it, it's the sort of incident farces are written round. There isn't any more of that stuff you put in my tea, is there? Or without the tea?"

Liz shook her head.

"Perhaps you're right." Margaret grimaced. "That would give Keith an excuse, wouldn't it? Me becoming a . . . lush? That is the word?"

"I believe so. What was she doing at the surgery?"

"Oh, that really is the best bit. Remember me telling you about the stables, the place where they breed show jumpers? Oh, very grand! Well, Miss Lydia Jennings is the owner. You see, not only has she got looks and personality, she's got money. She's not short on attributes. I don't know whether that makes me feel worse, or better," Margaret said dryly. Pushing herself from the armchair, she began to pace the room.

"Is she more attractive?"

Margaret came to a halt. "Of course! Haven't I just said? She's younger, for a start."

Liz smiled. "That doesn't always follow. Margaret, turn around. There's a mirror behind you. Just take a look in it."

For a moment Margaret stared back in disbelief, then she swivelled on her heel, slowly.

"See?" Liz came to stand behind her. "Your husband didn't even recognise you that day, did he?"

Briefly, Margaret smiled, but then she shook her head.

"Isn't that the point? This is how I am now. It's too late. Keith has gone. This . . . " She spread her hands, eyeing the woman in the mirror. "It's all about ten years too late. I miss him, Liz. Oh, I don't know if I'd have him back, even if he wanted to come. I'm not really certain whether what I feel isn't simply humiliation. He rejected me! Like an old car that's done good service but has to make way for a newer model, he threw me on the scrap heap."

Disgust edged each word, and Liz put an arm round her shoulders. "You've got to forget him. Get him out of your system, out of your mind. Think of him as dead."

"I've tried!" Petulantly Margaret stamped her foot. "Heavens! How I've tried. And I thought I'd done it, until today. Seeing that woman . . . I hated her, Liz. I really hated her."

Margaret tore herself away from Liz, struggling for composure.

"I like my work. I enjoy helping John; even Matthew Sayers. I've got to admit he's a good vet. And I've learned to make allowances, now I know about his wife. After all, it must be easier for me, at least I can hate Keith, but he, poor man, what can he do? No wonder he's morose.

"But you're right. I have made something of myself, and my life. I won't let that girl drive me away."

"I should think not!" Liz cried. "Just remember, if ever you two should meet again, that Keith lost something, too. Make up your mind that you don't need him."

"I'll try. But, I don't seem very good at making up my mind and sticking to it, these days."

"You're doing fine!"

Margaret smiled, weakly. "You can say that when the first time anything happens I don't come running to cry on your shoulder. Though I do appreciate it, Liz."

"Go on with you! I always understood that was what friends were for."

Margaret turned and gave Liz a quick hug. "Thanks! At least now I can drive home without killing anyone, or myself. I'm over this one."

However, walking into the empty house Margaret wasn't as sure of that as she'd tried to sound. She went through to the kitchen, plugging in the kettle before realising that she wasn't thirsty. She gazed about her, hating the cold orderliness of the room which spoke of its lone occupancy. Turning swiftly she ran upstairs, shedding her coat as she pushed open the bedroom door.

It was only as she saw the double bed she'd shared with Keith that she realised she'd come into the wrong room. Her fingers clenched into fists and she bit at the gleaming white knuckles. This wasn't her room, any more than this was her home.

Once she had lived here. Once she had been a wife and mother. Perhaps she was still a mother, in name, but she was no longer a wife.

"Who am I kidding," she whispered, "I'm not free! I never will be free of the past, and Keith, and all the years we shared together. Not while I live here where everything reminds me of him."

Closing the door quietly, but firmly,

behind her she made her way to the room where she had slept for the last months. This was her room. She had made it so; choosing the furniture from the rooms which had been Tracy's and Ian's. The bed cover was new, its pattern of lilac and white a bright splash of colour against the white headboard.

A tremor, as of excitement, tingled through her veins. There was no reason why she shouldn't make the rest of the house hers; root out the things which held memories; lay the ghost of Keith. Or . . . ?

She gasped at the thought which followed quickly.

Why not leave this house? Instead of trying to erase Keith, why not find a new place, something which would be completely hers from the start?

Tugging open the drawers she searched for a slip of paper she had pushed out of sight some weeks before when Keith had written, giving her a telephone number where she could contact him.

She dialled with fingers which didn't tremble.

"Keith? It's me!"

"Margaret? Is something wrong? Tracy?"

"No, everything's fine! Just fine! Keith, I'd like you to come round. I've decided we ought to sell this place."

"But, Margaret . . . "

"It's too big for me. Besides, I want something more convenient. I haven't time to waste on travelling backwards and forwards, nor on domesticity."

He started to protest but she cut him short.

"I would have thought you'd be glad. The upkeep on this house must be crippling. Look, come round, and we'll discuss what you want of the stuff here. The rest I'll sell and we can divide the proceeds down the middle. There's nothing to be gained in arguing, Keith, I've made up my mind."

"Well . . . I never intended, never planned . . . "

"There are things I never planned,

Keith. They just happened. I've learned that life's like that. What about coming Saturday?" she asked, having allowed her other remarks to sink in. "About eleven?"

She pressed the receiver down on its cradle, holding it there, as her previous elation ebbed away. Could she go through with this? She looked around the home which she'd loved and cared for for so many years, remembering where she'd bought a picture, what event had been marked by a vase.

Could she discard it all, her memories, everything? Yes, she could! She must! For only that way could she start a new life, taking none of the old heartaches with her.

Keith was standing on the path, looking uncertainly around him, when Margaret answered his ring the next Saturday. He didn't notice the door open at first, and Margaret watched his eyes widen as he took in her appearance. Then startled recognition lit his face.

"It was you? That day at the Red Lion?"

"Yes."

"Won't you come in?" Margaret stood back and Keith stepped into the hall.

"Tracy said you'd just left. I never thought . . ."

"Tracy?" Margaret halted. "So that was . . ." why she tried to delay me, Margaret finished the sentence silently.

"That was what?"

"Nothing! Didn't she tell you about the baby, Keith?"

"Oh, you mean . . . I see!"

"I wish I did. I'm not even sure why she came to see me. Tracy's gone her own way for years. She's never asked for advice. What has my life to do with her now? Or yours?"

Margaret poured tea from the silver pot which had been a wedding present.

Keith shifted in his chair, uneasily.

"Look here, Margaret. What is all this about selling? This is your home. I told you that."

"It was *our* home. Apparently, you no longer want it, well, neither do I.

"I don't want the furniture, the carpets, anything! We sell, and divide the money, as I said. That way I can get the kind of place I do want."

"But, you loved all these things." Keith waved round the room. "You loved decorating and fixing things up."

"Maybe I did, but not any longer. Keith, I don't understand why you're arguing. I didn't think there was anything in this house that you valued."

She watched him wince, but he didn't speak.

"So! You must decide what you want. I'll arrange the sale, both of the house and the furnishings. Just let me know what I mustn't send to the sale-room, when you've had time to think."

She had moved into the hall by now and, perforce, Keith had followed her. As she stood, her hand on the outside door, she felt Keith's eyes run over her.

It was the sort of look she had noticed in other men's eyes recently, but she hadn't seen it in Keith's for some time. She smiled, standing poised, conscious that she was slim and desirable.

"You've changed, Margaret," Keith said, at last, his eyes coming back to her face. "Oh, it's not just . . ." He sketched in the new hairstyle, the slim figure, the long legs and strappy sandals. And as she continued to hold his gaze he shifted uncomfortably.

"You're quite . . . well, different," he ended, his cheeks flaming. And they both knew what he had almost said.

★ ★ ★

Flat hunting, Margaret discovered, was exciting and tiring, and she sighed when the front door bell rang one evening just as she was preparing a bed time drink.

When she opened the door, her daughter-in-law, Janet, almost knocked her over as she strode inside.

172

"You're not going to bed, are you?"

"Not to sleep. Would you like some coffee?"

"Mother! This isn't a social call."

"No," Margaret spoke quietly. "I can see it isn't. But you might as well come through."

As they reached the sitting-room Janet spoke.

"What right had you to interfere in my life? Oh, yes! I soon guessed Ian had been round here."

"Janet, I think you'd better calm down."

"I'm not going to regret what I came to say, Mother-in-law. Ian's happy where he is. We have a good life. He doesn't need this other job. Dragging me away to some God-forsaken place."

"If Ian is happy, why did he apply for the job? But, you're wrong, I didn't tell Ian to go. He's a grown man. He's old enough to make up his own mind. In fact, I suspect that's exactly what he has done. I'm sorry his decision doesn't please you, but that's between the two of you."

"Don't you care that he's taking little Vicky away? Don't you mind that your son won't be near? I should have thought you'd want him to stay here, the way things have turned out."

Margaret flinched. "Janet, the way things have turned out, I've discovered it isn't easy to keep anyone where they don't wish to be. I should remember that, if I were you."

For a moment Janet was silent. When she did speak there were tears in her voice.

"Don't you care about Vicky? You do know the kind of people he'll be teaching?"

"Ian told me. I don't think you need worry about Vicky, but, yes, I will miss her. Now, I'm sorry, Janet — but I have a busy day at the surgery tomorrow."

Reluctantly, Janet followed her to the door and there she turned, looking Margaret up and down, just as Keith had done. But this time the look was different, less complimentary.

"You've changed. You're not like you used to be. You're not gentle, not like an ordinary mother, at all."

Margaret leaned against the door when she'd closed it. Twice within the space of a few days she had been accused of changing, almost as if she'd committed some crime.

Yes, she thought. I was ordinary, Janet. Ordinary, like a doormat.

8

"**I**S that the last?" Matthew Sayers flipped through the appointment book on Margaret's desk. "Thank goodness for that. No more patients until the afternoon session, and John should be in by then, shouldn't he?"

"I expect so. Yes, he said that."

Margaret turned from the filing cabinet as she heard a long sigh behind her, to find Matthew Sayers perched on the edge of her desk, his long legs stretched across her path.

He was rubbing his eyes, lines of strain creasing his forehead and Margaret felt a stab of sympathy.

"I'll make some coffee, shall I?" she suggested, compassionately.

The vet lifted his head. "Please! I'm dead beat. I was called out last night."

"Oh!" Margaret glanced over her

shoulder as she filled the kettle. "I never thought of vets getting called out like human doctors."

"Vets aren't human?"

Margaret stiffened, turning slowly to face him. "I'm sorry. I simply meant that doctors treat humans, they're not animal doctors."

Her voice trailed away as she realised Matthew was looking at her, his face troubled.

"I was joking. You know — making a funny, as my daughter would phrase it."

"Oh! Oh, yes! Yes, of course, Mr Sayers."

Margaret swung back to her task, biting her lip, conscious that his eyes were still on her.

"I expect it's like a lot of things," he said, thoughtfully, after a moment. "It takes practice."

Margaret frowned. The words didn't make sense. She turned to face him.

"I'm sorry?"

"Joking. It takes practice," the vet

explained, painstakingly. "I suppose one gets out of the habit."

The kettle hissed as it boiled and Margaret was glad of the excuse to attend to it. She filled a cup and handed it to Matthew.

"Aren't you having one?" he asked, cradling both hands round the cup, making Margaret think of Ian when he was a boy.

"No! No, not now. I, I'd better get tidied up," she muttered, backing towards the treatment rooms. She knew she had to get away. If she stayed talking, let that feeling of sympathy blot out her commonsense, she knew she would say something she would regret. She pulled on an overall as she entered the room, aware that Matthew had got to his feet also, but she sighed with relief when she heard him close the door of his office. Though there was a hint of bitterness in the sigh.

If John had been here he would have stayed chatting, telling her something of the various small operations he'd performed. He might even have tried to help, until Margaret ordered him to sit down, out of her way. But Matthew Sayers had never volunteered his services, never spoken of treatments.

As she collected the instruments to be sterilised she went over the last few minutes. I muffed it, she thought. The first time he's shown a crack in that armour of his and I muffed it. Standing there like a dim-wit, while he explained that he'd been joking. How must he have felt? No wonder the poor man can't relax. If anyone ought to understand what he's gone through, I should.

Idiot! Idiot that I am.

She pulled back the lid of the rather ancient steriliser and slotted the tray of instruments into place. It appeared to catch, then, as she let go, it slipped. Instinctively, she grabbed for the handles, forgetful of the hot water, and as it seared her flesh she cried out. The tears starting in her eyes she backed away, holding her wrist, keeping her fingers stretched stiffly as she moaned with pain.

Suddenly Matthew was beside her, one hand catching her arm, the other round her body as he propelled her towards the washbasin. She made to protest as he turned on the cold tap and thrust her hand under it, but as the cold water brought relief she relaxed.

"Why on earth didn't you watch what you were doing? You could have been hurt."

"I was," Margaret whispered, mock heroically. "And I did watch. It slipped. You don't think I did it on purpose, do you?"

"You shouldn't have tried to catch it. That was stupid," Matthew told her, and Margaret flashed him a look. She hadn't realised he'd been watching her.

"It was instinctive. People normally try to catch something if they drop it. Or don't you ever behave like other people?" she asked, scathingly.

Matthew didn't as much let go of

her wrist as toss it away, and Margaret, after a moment, brought it clear of the rushing water. It didn't look too bad, and though it stung she decided she would live.

"We'd better get it fixed up."

"It'll be all right. The steriliser wasn't switched on. It wasn't boiling water. It's all right now. It doesn't hurt much."

"Then why are you crying?"

"Because, because . . . " Margaret brushed the tears from her cheeks with her uninjured hand. "I don't know! Shock, I suppose. And I'm not crying."

"You're not?" Matthew stepped closer. "Then, what's this?"

Gently his finger touched her cheek, catching a tear as it overflowed.

"I'm sorry I shouted at you. Natural reaction, I expect, like you grabbing for the tray. In that way I do behave like other people. I get alarmed and upset when accidents happen. Then I shout."

"I'm sorry," Margaret whispered.

Matthew was bending over her.

Somehow, she had found her way to a chair, or he'd led her there, she wasn't quite sure. But, however it had been achieved, his face was close to hers, his eyes studying her face with concern. Margaret wished he'd go away. Wished he'd, at least, move out of touching distance. Just until she could master the insane desire to run her finger over the lips which were smiling gently down at her.

"No, I'm the one who should apologise," Matthew said, quietly. "Fancy bawling you out when you were already in pain. *I'm* sorry."

He took the handkerchief from his breast pocket and, as Margaret sat, too bewildered by events to resist, he began to wipe away her tears, resting a hand on her shoulder as he did so.

Margaret scarcely felt the light touch on her cheeks, but where his fingers lay on her arm the flesh seemed to tingle. A strange desire to lay her head against him rose up in her; an ache to feel the roughness of his jacket under her cheek almost overtook her. Almost, but not quite. As Matthew stood back, smiling down at her, she closed her eyes quickly, fearful that he might read the emotions there. Then, bending her head, keeping her eyes from his, she made to rise.

"Margaret!" The hand which had steadied her, moved to press her back against the chair. "Sit still! You've had a shock."

Alarmed by the intensity of emotion his touch evoked, Margaret pushed his hand away, brusquely.

"I'm all right! Don't fuss!"

Instantly the smile left Matthew's face and he thrust his hands deep into the pockets of his white coat.

"I'm sorry." He swung on his heel. "I'll make some coffee. You wouldn't have any objection to me doing that, will you?"

He flung the words over his shoulder as he strode to the outer office.

Margaret shuddered, though her

hand scarcely pained her now, it was her heart that was hurt. And her pride, she realised. You thought you were strong, emancipated, an inward voice taunted her. After Keith left you imagined you'd never experience such feelings again. In fact, you were determined you wouldn't. And, let's face it. You haven't felt like that for a long time.

A very long time, she added, bitterly, recalling the months before Keith's desertion. Only now realising how little love and affection there had been between them for sometime. But Matthew was probably laughing at her now. He must have recognised the effect he'd had on her.

Oh, God! What must he think of me?

She heard a step and lifted her head to see Matthew staring at her from the other side of the desk. There was a cup in his hands and, as she watched, he placed the cup, with arm outstretched, meticulously in front of her.

Margaret flushed, mastering the urge to shout that he needn't be scared. She wouldn't allow her guard to drop again, not now she knew.

"Thank you. But, I am better now. I'll get back to work."

"Sit down!"

The barked words took the bit of strength she'd summoned from Margaret's legs.

"Mr Sayers?" she whispered.

"I said, sit down . . . before you fall down. I can finish up in here."

"But, Mr Sayers, it's my job."

"We don't employ you to kill yourself. Oh, I know!" He waved aside her protestations. "You're not badly hurt. But you might have been. You made a silly mistake. And before you argue, and in spite of what I might have implied in the past, I don't think you are normally careless. I suspect you're tired, or upset, or . . . whatever. I also suspect that you'll say it's none of my business. But I would rather you didn't do anything else to hurt yourself whilst

I'm around. Animals in pain I can just about cope with, but people!"

He smiled, shamefacedly, spreading his hands in a helpless gesture.

"My wife was . . . sick, for rather a long time, before she died."

His voice was so low Margaret could only just hear the words and she held her breath, fearful she might shatter this moment.

"So . . . just leave things to me . . . will you?"

"Yes, yes of course, Mr Sayers."

Matthew watched her relax, taking up the coffee and drinking it, sip, sip, sip; like a dutiful child. But as he turned away, Margaret thought she caught the glimpse of a smile, and his voice held a note of amusement when he spoke.

"And, Margaret, do you think you could bring yourself to call me Matthew?"

★ ★ ★

186

John Andrews tut-tutted when he learned the reason for the dressing on Margaret's hand.

"I'm a silly old fool. I should have let Matthew have his way and bought something more modern. But," he eyed her, questioningly.

"Some good seems to have come out of it. You and Matthew are friendlier."

Margaret shrugged. "The cure seems a bit drastic. I certainly don't intend trying anything like that again."

"Let's hope there'll be no need," John said, as if she'd been serious. "It's a couple of years since Matthew's wife died. It's time he took up with life again.

"Margaret, these last years haven't been easy for Matthew. You, of all people, should know how hard it is to come to terms with losing someone."

Margaret's head shot up, and for a moment she faced John defiantly, until she remembered that he didn't know the truth.

"John, it is, wasn't, like you think,

like I led you to believe. I'm not a widow, John, no matter what I implied. I expect the truth wasn't quite as palatable. Keith . . . my husband, walked out on me. It's as simple as that."

"My dear . . . I."

Margaret held up her hand, warding off sympathy. "It's over now. I've adjusted. But, Matthew . . . How can I say what the future might hold? I need to be free, to get to know myself, to know who there is under the façade which was Keith's wife. Don't you see?"

"Yes. But, ultimately, we all need someone. I guessed you were lonely and I'd like to say, now, that I'm here, your friend, if you need me. And Matthew too, I'm sure. Will you remember that?"

Margaret nodded and after a slight hesitation John walked to his room. But at the door he halted.

"How's Barney? Did those tablets do the trick?"

On safer ground Margaret spoke eagerly. "I'm sure they did. But he still chokes, as if there was something there." She touched her own throat.

"He was badly infected. Why don't you bring him in again? Check my schedule and fix a time, eh?"

"I will, and thank you . . . for everything."

But that evening she had little time to worry about Barney, glad that he ate his food with little difficulty.

"Good boy!" she told him. "Now you stay there. I've got to get into my best bib and tucker. I'm having a visitor," she grinned, wishing Barney could share the joke.

Her husband was due in an hour.

Having found a flat Margaret had rung him, suggesting he came over and decide what he wanted from the house.

"There are some things which are strictly yours. I wouldn't want to throw anything out you valued," she had told him.

Now, after a quick shower, she slipped into a cream, linen-look, sheath dress, fixing large brown studs into her ears.

Fastening the buckles of her slim-heeled sandals she took a last, morale boosting, look at herself in the mirror.

"Not bad!" she smiled. "Now don't you keep me waiting, Keith," she prayed as a flutter of panic brought her hand to her heart.

She breathed deeply, and when the doorbell pealed she walked with firm steps to answer it.

"Not late am I?" Keith's voice was a shade too hearty as he followed her through to the sitting-room.

"I've put the things I thought you might want in the breakfast room. Take whatever you like, then the rest can go to the sales room."

"You've got it all planned."

"Someone had to."

His eyes closed, and as she watched, the colour ran up into his cheeks making him look as bashful as a small boy. She wanted to tell him she hadn't meant to sound angry. She felt an urge to touch his cheek, to brush back the hair from his forehead.

"Keith!" Anger at herself sharpened her tone. "I don't want this to take all night."

"Okay! Okay!" Keith sidled away and Margaret collapsed into a chair, trembling.

Sometime later Keith called her name.

"What is it?"

"This." Keith came to the door, a small glass figure in his hand. It shone, catching the light, changing from blue to green, as he turned it, and Margaret's fingers clenched, her mind running back to the workshop in Venice.

They had watched the man make the figure, and the dying rays of the sun had caught the colours then. Keith had translated what the workman had said.

'As blue as the eyes of your beautiful lady.'

And Keith had kissed her, there and then, before all the other patrons crowding the room. But, they were on their honeymoon, and perhaps it showed. For, nowhere else in all the world, was a lover loved as in Italy.

"No!" She spoke harshly. "No, I don't want it."

"I see."

For a second their glances held until Keith turned away.

Margaret walked quickly through to the kitchen. Why? Why, did he still have to try to hurt her? What had she done to deserve it? She was drinking black coffee when Keith came back in from loading his car.

"I, I think that's all. I suppose I'd better be going.

"Er . . . see you!" he cried when she simply nodded.

But before the door was fully closed he pushed it open again.

"Margaret, have you seen Tracy lately? She seemed upset, worried, or something."

"Women are apt to worry over their first child. Don't you remember?"

"Perhaps. But I think she'd appreciate a talk with you."

Margaret laughed shortly. "When did Tracy ever listen to a word I said? But okay, if she asks me . . . I'll see what I can do."

"Talking of Tracy," Keith teetered on the balls of his feet. "Could I have some photographs, do you think? Just one or two?"

Margaret's stomach contracted but she spoke evenly enough. "Of course!"

She slid from her stool, leading the way back to the sitting-room, pulling a couple of large albums from a cupboard. "Take the lot," she ordered.

"No, of course not! I just want a couple. I could get copies, then you can have them back."

She went back to her cooling coffee, not wanting to watch him reviewing the past they'd shared. But when at last he'd driven away she ran to pick up the albums.

Turning the pages she checked what Keith had taken. Several of the children, charting their progress through the years. One of his mother who had died some months before Keith had left. And a view or two. Nothing more. None of her, nor of the times they'd shared. Margaret sat on, pain gathering like a hot ball in her chest. How long? How long would it be before Keith lost the power to hurt her? Would the scars ever heal?

The shopping precinct was bathed in sunshine as Margaret threaded her way across it through the crowds of shoppers.

Once Barney had finished his medication she had checked on John's first free period, and this afternoon she was on her way to Liz Short's to collect him.

The little dog seemed no worse, but not much better either and she was placing all her faith on John Andrews, wishing there was someone who would understand and share her burden. Liz tried, but she had never kept a pet herself so had no idea how they could creep into one's heart.

And everyone else is wrapped up in their own troubles, she thought, recalling the conversation she'd had only the evening before with Ian.

Apparently, he had rung to apologise for his wife's visit, but as that had been some days before, Margaret thought the pretext was a little thin. More probably, he wanted to discuss things with someone he felt was on his side.

"And has Janet agreed?" she asked, when Ian had apologised, more than sufficiently.

Ian didn't speak for a moment, then, in a new, hard voice which she scarcely recognised as that of her easy going son, he said, "I've told Janet I'm taking the job. Mother, I've never been so sure of anything in my life, as I am over this. You agreed I should decide for myself."

"And Janet? Is she happier? Does she want you to take it?"

"She hasn't decided, not yet. But, *I'm* going. If Janet comes with me, I'll be glad, but . . . I'm going."

Now Margaret wondered if she'd been right to speak at all. She still believed her advice had been sound, but if it led to Ian and Janet splitting up? Wasn't it sufficient trauma for young Vicky that her grandparents no longer lived in the same house?

Suddenly, her thoughts were jerked back to the present as she heard her name called.

"Margaret! It is Margaret, isn't it?" the woman asked, a little breathless from having run after her.

"Yes, but . . . " Margaret eyed the young woman. She didn't think she'd ever met her before, yet the woman knew her name. Perhaps they were acquainted.

"I'm sorry," she began, and the woman smiled, shyly.

"No, that's all right. I'm the one who should be sorry, but I don't know your surname. They didn't use them . . . at the group therapy meeting . . . Remember?"

Margaret flushed. Yes, she remembered. Not that she wanted to do.

"I only went once."

"Mmm! Pity really. You spoke well. But, of course, you didn't need help. You were . . . Look, I'm sorry, but I felt I couldn't let you walk past, once I'd recognised you. I've often wished I could thank you. You helped me that day. Don't you remember? You told me to take up my own life, to do something that I used to enjoy. Well, I did, and . . . "

Margaret watched the other woman's eyes fall, and she hastened to put her at ease.

"I'm glad what I said helped. Though I can't think what you must all have thought of me, shooting off my mouth that way," she grinned.

"No, you did right to speak. You were right. And, well, I for one took your advice. Oh, the whole world didn't change overnight, but I am happier. So

. . . I just had to tell you."

Margaret smiled. "I'm glad. You certainly look well."

"And you. You look terrific!"

They stood a moment, eyeing each other nervously, uncertain how to make the break now. Then, a child, running to get close to the fountain in the centre of the square, dashed between them.

"It's a lovely day, isn't it?" Margaret said, her voice falsely bright. "But I must be off. I've got to collect my car from the garage."

"Yes, and I must go too. Bye! Bye!" the woman called, already some paces away.

Margaret watched her go, her spirits rising. Perhaps she hadn't been wrong to talk to Ian. Someone had benefited from advice she'd offered. So I can't be wrong all the time, she thought.

The car was waiting, clean, and purring softly once more, and Margaret slid into the driving seat, her thoughts returning to Barney.

Liz was waiting for her, the dog on her knee, and Margaret dropped on to the rug before him.

"How is he? How's he been?"

"Just the same," Liz answered. "I think you're wise to take him in."

Gently Margaret gathered Barney into her arms. "John said not to worry, so I'm sure he's going to be all right."

"Margaret." Liz stopped her as she made to leave. "Did you do anything about what your . . . what Keith said? About ringing Tracy?"

Margaret's expression hardened. "No."

"I think you should, my dear. If he noticed something . . . Men aren't given to noticing things, are they?" she smiled.

"Maybe not. Oh, okay! I suppose I could ring her. Yes, all right. I will. Sometime. I must be off now. Come on, old fellow. We're going for a ride."

The dog recognised the phrase and as his tail thumped slightly against

Margaret she felt more confident. He was going to get well.

But when she tapped on John's door it was Matthew's which opened.

"John's had to go out, I'm afraid. An emergency, and I was tied up."

"Will he be long? I don't mind waiting."

Matthew looked down at the dog in her arms. "It's doubtful if he'll even come back. If he's very late he might well go on home. Look, why don't you bring him through, Margaret?"

He stood back but Margaret hesitated. She wanted to find out how Barney really was, but she had set her hopes on John. However, she knew it wouldn't be fair on the dog to put it off any longer.

"Thanks," she said, belatedly and carried Barney to the examination table, surprised to find that it was already prepared. Matthew hadn't expected her to refuse.

Once Barney was asleep the vet began to run his hands over him, his eyes thoughtful, but his expression betraying nothing.

"How long has he been like this, listless, I mean?"

"A month, two . . . He is getting old."

She leaned forward as the vet opened Barney's mouth, taking a spatula to hold down his tongue. But Matthew's head came between her and the light he was shining into the dog's jaws.

"Did John give you any indication of what he thought it might be?"

"He said Barney's throat was badly infected."

Matthew stretched upright, tossing the spatula into the bin.

"You know," Margaret breathed. "You do know, what's wrong."

"I'm afraid so. I believe . . . "

He got no further as the door opened and John walked in. After a glance into Matthew's face John came to take Margaret's hands.

"I'm sorry, my dear. I meant to be here."

"I know. Matthew's examined Barney," she began, but John silenced her, pressing her fingers.

"What do you think, Matthew?"

"Take a look."

Margaret moved forward too, her fingers gripping the edge of the table. As John straightened she clutched his arm.

"He's going to be all right, isn't he? Those tablets, they've helped. If he has some more . . . ?"

"I don't think . . . " John faced Matthew. "Those new injections that Rep recommended would probably relieve the symptoms, Matthew."

"John!" Matthew's voice cut through Margaret's sigh of relief. "You know there's only one injection that animal needs."

"No!" The word was a whimper and John looked towards Margaret as she sank on to a stool. He couldn't forget the conversation they'd had earlier. Barney was all she had.

"Barney's my patient, Matthew. I

think the decision must be mine."

Matthew tore the gloves from his hands. "Yes, he's your patient. I've given you my opinion, the rest is up to you, as you say."

"But . . . But, Barney's not that sick. Coming here he was looking through the car window, just like he always used to," Margaret cried.

Matthew swung round, his face suffused with anger.

"Used to, Margaret. Can't you understand? Or won't you? Are you thinking of that poor animal, or not? Do you love him? Really love him? Enough to make the right decision?"

"John?"

Margaret turned anguished eyes towards him and John found it hard to meet his partner's gaze.

How could he tell this distraught woman that Matthew was right? How could he say that she must lose her pet, her friend? Could he take from her the only thing she appeared to have left? She trusted him now, just as she had trusted him that day when she had spoken of her husband's desertion. He couldn't betray either trust.

"We can try, my dear. We can see what the injections will do."

There was an angry exclamation from Matthew and when they turned, he was tearing off his coat.

"Yes, you can try. But don't ask me to be a party to this . . . this travesty! I thought better of you, John, and . . . "

His eyes seared into Margaret's face until she dropped her head to escape them. When the door slammed shut behind him, she spoke, her voice a mere whisper.

"He despises me. He thinks I'm selfish, uncaring . . . He . . . " She couldn't go on, and as John's arms came round her she collapsed against him, the tears scorching her throat.

But she wasn't crying for Barney alone, but from the knowledge that it mattered to her what Matthew Sayers thought of her.

9

"JOHN." Margaret lifted her head, forcing back her sobs. It did matter to her what Matthew thought. She couldn't allow him to go on thinking she didn't care enough for Barney to put his needs first.

"John," she began again. "Is Matthew right?" She caught the swift change in John's expression and didn't wait for his answer, as another thought struck her. Why had John and Matthew differed over the necessary treatment for the sick animal? They were both excellent, caring vets. Why hadn't their diagnosis been the same? Such a thing had never happened before, to her knowledge.

"I'm right, aren't I? You do agree with him? Then, why? Why did you say you'd give Barney those other injections?"

"Because . . . Don't you see, Margaret? You talked to me, told me how things were. I understand, perhaps more than Matthew, just what Barney means to you."

"But, if Barney's sick, very sick, then wouldn't it be best . . . ?"

She could get no further as John's hands clasped hers firmly.

"Perhaps a few months longer," he said, quietly. "Perhaps then you'll be more able to cope."

"But you would have agreed, you do agree with Matthew?"

Slowly John nodded, and Margaret echoed the action.

Without another word she turned and walked towards Matthew's room, and after rapping lightly on the door pushed it open. The younger vet was standing staring out into the street, but even from the set of his shoulders, Margaret guessed he was still very angry. He didn't appear to have heard the door open and she took a step or two towards him.

"Matthew, I, . . . I just came to say that I know you're right."

He had turned as she began speaking and his first sight of her brought an angry frown to his forehead. But, as she continued to speak his expression changed to one of bewilderment.

"I just had to tell you. I see, now, how selfish I was."

She didn't wait for Matthew's reaction to this but turned quickly, fumbling for the door through eyes blurred with tears. In the other room, she brushed past John, and went through to the reception area. John came to stand by the door, watching her. As she picked up her handbag she spoke.

"You'll take care of Barney for me, won't you, John? I couldn't bear . . . Please, John, look after him."

She had gone, the outside door swinging behind her, before John could reassure her, and, after a moment, he moved back into the treatment room where the little dog was just beginning to wake.

The street was busy as Margaret came out into the bright spring evening, and as the strolling crowds jostled her she turned impatiently, seeking somewhere where she could be relatively alone. Across the road she caught a glimpse of trees and recalled the park she had noticed but never had time to explore.

Unheeding of the traffic she ran towards its sanctuary.

Here, too, there were people, but turning away from the main path which wound its way through the park, Margaret felt her feet sink into the earth and the smell of damp grass filled her nostrils, reminding her of other evenings when Barney had gambolled beside her.

How he had loved his walks, even up to a short while ago he had plodded behind her, taking a few running steps to catch up now and again. Margaret's breath caught in her throat. Why hadn't she noticed then? Why hadn't she read the signs? Matthew was right. She'd been too immersed in her own troubles to care. But could that be true? She loved Barney. And hadn't it been he who had helped her through those first weeks after Keith's departure?

But, treacherously, her mind returned to the morning she had discovered him locked in the kitchen, his food and drink bowls empty. Oh, Barney! How could I? Heedlessly, she walked on, the sights and scenes around her unnoticed, intruding only when circumstances brought them within her vision. A child chasing a ball. Birds fluttering upwards from under her feet. The thud of bat on ball from the nearby cricket pitch. And, overall, the shouts of children, and the chatter of adults when they passed close by.

She had walked almost to the perimeter of the park before she realised and, shortening her stride, she turned back, moving to circle the children's area, with its swings and sand-pit, searching for an empty bench.

Finding one, a little way back from the play area, she sat, the pain easing a little as she watched the children. There had been a park, similar to this, where she had brought Tracy and Ian, when they were smaller.

Tracy had been ten when they'd bought Barney. Keith having said that the children must be old enough to take care of a pet before they got one.

Would they miss Barney now? She doubted it. They both had their own lives, and since they had gone away to college had seen the little dog as simply a part of the lives they had once led. As if against a sudden blow, Margaret felt her heart contract. How would she survive without him? Now there would be no one to welcome her home, no one to talk to. For, even though he couldn't answer in words, Barney appeared to understand. He knew when she was sad, and crawled into her lap, whimpering his sympathy. When she was happy he would leap about her, giving sharp little barks, enjoying the excitement.

Margaret pulled up her thoughts, angrily. What was she doing, thinking in the present? These were all things Barney had done. Things he would never do again. What did it matter that she was shortly to move into a brand new, modern flat? That she had picked herself up after Keith's desertion; not only picked herself up but fashioned a new, more satisfying life for herself? What did all that mean? Yes, she was more alive, attractive, confident, than she had ever been, but of what value was it all?

Nothing, she decided, if there was no one to share it.

Matthew? She had driven Matthew away. The scorn in his voice, the look in his eyes when she had rejected his advice, proved that he would want nothing more to do with her. Even the fact that she had told him he had been right couldn't change that. Her body felt empty, as empty as the life she saw ahead. This was almost worse than when Keith had left. Now, she couldn't even cry.

She shivered, and realised that she must have been sitting there for some time and the evening dew was falling. Despite the earlier sunshine, summer hadn't arrived yet. Slowly she started to get to her feet, only partly aware that someone had sat down beside her.

"Margaret." The name, spoken quietly, scarcely penetrated into her conscious mind, and she took a step away.

"Margaret! Wait!"

She turned then, recognising the voice, but yet not believing what her ears told her. "Matthew?"

"Matthew? Is . . . ? There's something wrong?"

"No! At least, not the way you mean. The only thing that's wrong is me. Me and my infernal temper, and lack of thought or . . . consideration. Sit down, please, Margaret," he added, as she hesitated. "I've got to talk to you."

Margaret sank on to the bench, clenching her hands in her lap, sure that Matthew had come to tell her something bad. Though what, she couldn't imagine.

She kept her eyes fastened on her twisting fingers. "Barney?" she asked quietly. Matthew's hand came to lie across hers. "Barney's fine, now. John did what you asked."

She nodded, unable to speak, and Matthew's grip tightened.

"Why did you come?" Margaret asked, after a moment.

"I thought we were friends. I hoped we were at least that, Margaret. Don't you need a friend just now?"

Again Margaret nodded, but this time a slight raising of the corners of her mouth indicated she wanted to smile.

Matthew lifted his hand to touch her cheek, gently, and feeling the tear which had spilled over her lashes he slipped his arm around her shoulders, bringing her head to lie against him. It was the motivation Margaret's wrought emotions needed. With a strangled sound she began to weep.

Matthew held her quietly for some minutes, but gradually he began to talk.

"John told me about your husband. Told me, too, why he had backed up your decision. I was a fool. I ought to have known John wouldn't go against all he's ever believed in without some good reason. But . . . I told you once that I could cope with pain in animals; that's not strictly true. I suppose the fact that I can't is why I became a vet. Seeing Barney, knowing that he was suffering and that he might suffer even more, I suppose I couldn't see anything else. My emotions got in the way of my sense. I should have known you wouldn't act selfishly. I've watched you work, seen your compassion. I ought to have looked deeper."

Margaret's sobs were easing, and as she stirred, Matthew took a large handkerchief from his pocket and lifted her chin with the point of his finger. Then, smiling tenderly, he wiped away the stains on her cheeks.

"I do understand, my dear. I do know what it's like to lose someone. The pain, the loneliness, the feeling that no one under . . . "

He got not further. Margaret straightened, moving away from his ministrations.

"No, Matthew, I know you mean well, but I don't think you do understand. Clearly, it must have been terrible when your wife died, and the time before when she was sick and you had to sit by, knowing what must happen. But, afterwards . . . No, it wasn't the same. When Keith walked out of my life he took my confidence, the life I had grown used to, even my children's affection, for a time. He rejected me. He threw back in my face the years we'd had, the love I'd had for him, the care and attention I'd given him. He'd degraded me. Yes," she added, thoughtfully. "That's exactly what he did. I was down graded, no longer something to be cherished but, like a packet of food in a supermarket that has passed its sell-by date, I had lost value. Can you understand what that did to me?"

"Yes, Yes, I think I can. But, you survived, Margaret. You're back on top. You've got everything going for you, as they say these days. You're young, attractive, you've got work that you obviously enjoy, and . . . you've got friends."

Margaret smiled as she heard the odd little emphasis he put on that last word.

"Yes," she agreed. "I've got friends. You being here, your jacket all damp and soggy, shows that I've one, at least."

"Margaret, I . . . "

She stopped him, putting a finger gently across his lips.

"Perhaps you're right. In fact, I know you are," she added, realising that Matthew hadn't known the woman she'd been, the one whom Keith had deserted . . .

"But if it takes two to make a marriage, it follows it needs two to break it, Matthew. You have nothing to blame yourself for, whilst I . . . "

"I can't believe . . . ," Matthew began. "But we were talking about Barney. When you asked about him, just now, I said he was fine. You understood what I meant. He's out of pain. Soon you'll be able to take comfort from that, just as I did."

Impulsively, Margaret turned to him, putting up her hands to cup his face.

"Dear, Matthew, I've been selfish, again. As if what I'm suffering was even a part of what you've gone through! Forgive me."

Matthew turned his face so that his lips touched the palm of her hand.

"Let's go for a coffee," he said, and taking her hands he chaffed them between his. "You're cold."

"Not really," she answered, pulling him to stand before her. "Somehow,

I get the impression there are warmer days ahead," she smiled.

★ ★ ★

"I think we ought to have a flat-warming party," Margaret told Liz, as they watched the empty removal van drive away from the flat. "Give the place a lived-in feel. What do you say?"

"If you mean one of those events where one ends up with cigarette burns in the upholstery and stains on the carpet, I say no."

"If those are the sort of friends you have, I'll be careful not to invite any of them," Margaret teased. "But, just because this is a flat instead of a house, I don't see why I shouldn't celebrate. Who shall we ask?"

"It's your party. Who do you want, besides Matthew?"

"I did think of inviting you, but I'm having second thoughts. There's John, of course; — you'll like him . . . "

"So I'm reprieved. I am to be allowed to come," Liz chuckled.

"Well, I suppose I'll have to ask you, after all the hard work you've put in today," Margaret tried to look doubtful.

"So think yourself lucky. Now! Where was I? John, you, Matthew, and of course Erica. I don't know how she'll feel being included with a lot of old fogies like us . . . "

"Speak for yourself! How do you get along with Matthew's daughter, by the way?"

"Mmm! That's a hard one. I haven't seen much of her, passing friends might be the phrase. But, she doesn't seem to resent me, or anything. Yes, I suppose you could say we're friends. That seems to be everyone." Margaret laughed, a little ruefully. "I don't seem to have a large social circle, do I? But most of the people I knew at one time were joint friends, couples, you know. Well, it'll just have to be dinner then. It'll be nicer that way, don't you think?

Now, all we've got to do is decide on a date; and what I'm to feed you all on."

"Is that all? Well, Margaret," Liz Short said, getting to her feet. "I didn't mind helping you out today. I'll even come and clean the silver, or what have you, for this dinner party, but don't expect me to cook. People talk about sliced bread as the greatest invention, to me it's frozen meals."

"Message received and understood! Please, dear friend, will you arrive here, in your best bib and tucker, of course, around seven o'clock, a week today? Say, seven to eat around half-past."

However, despite the proviso she'd made about helping Margaret prepare for her guests, Liz arrived at the flat around eleven on the following Saturday.

Margaret was already at work in the kitchen, surrounded by mounds of food in various stages of preparation. Liz took an apron from her shopping bag and donned it.

"Okay! Where do I start? Although I must say everywhere looks spick and span."

The smile with which Margaret had greeted her friend slipped from her face.

"It doesn't get dirty, not even untidy," she said, mournfully. "I'm out all day and there's no one . . . to . . . untidy it."

"Oh, don't tell me," she said, quickly, as Liz made to speak. "I'm not the only one. There are millions like me, I know. But I do miss having someone."

"Say it! It's Barney you're talking about, isn't it?"

"Don't you dislike coming back into an empty house, Liz?"

"I've had a bit longer to get used to it. And it wasn't quite as traumatic in my case. You will learn to live with it."

"I'm being a bore, aren't I? Look," Margaret said quickly. "If you have come to help you might make us a cup of coffee before anything else. Then, if you don't mind peeling vegetables . . . ?"

They worked happily together for some time, chatting amicably of this and that.

"How's Tracy," Liz asked, as they were laying the table, ready for the evening. "She'll be near her time, now, won't she?"

"Mmm!" Margaret surveyed the flowers she'd arranged as a centre piece. "About that . . . "

Her eyes lifted to her friend's face and her mouth gaped open as she realised what Liz had meant by her question.

"Oh, God!" she cried. "I didn't ring. I kept meaning to, but what with Barney, and moving here."

With a conscience stricken look she counted on her fingers. Then her face cleared.

"Oh, nearly seven months. She'll be okay. But, you're right, I ought to have checked. I'll do it now. There should be one of them in, it's almost lunch time."

Walking through to the kitchen she dialled Tracy's number, letting it ring several times before replacing the receiver.

"They must be out. I'll try again, later."

But though she rang a couple of times whilst she and Liz were eating the sandwiches she'd cut, there was still no answer.

"I'll try again, tomorrow. If they're out shopping, or something, she must be fit. Sunday, might be a better time to reach them."

Liz nodded. "I expect so. See you this evening, then."

Margaret followed her friend to the door. "Hurrah! Post." She bent to pick up the envelopes. "No bills. I expect they'll all come in an avalanche, later."

She shuffled the letters together as she opened the door. "See you tonight, love," she called.

Back in the living-room she thumbed through the mail again, dropping the numerous adverts into the waste paper basket as a bulging envelope caught her eye. She turned it over. The writing wasn't familiar and she peered at the date stamp. Plymouth! It must be from Ian. No wonder she hadn't recognised his hand, she hadn't received any letters from him since he'd been a young man at college, and then very seldom.

Eagerly she tore it open, glancing briefly at the wad of photographs before putting them aside.

'*Dear Mother*,' she read, surprise mounting as she realised it wasn't Ian who had written but Janet.

'*Ian wanted to write, but I thought I'd like to let you know how things were down here. Mum, we really love it. I know I said all those things, but I was wrong. It's not only that Ian is so much happier, doing work he enjoys, but that I've been brought into it, too. For the first time in my life; except maybe when Vicky was little and so* dependent on me; I feel needed! And valued! Please! I'm not saying that Ian didn't value me, it's not that. It's hard to explain, really. But, if you haven't looked at the snapshots yet, just do so. Just take a look at how happy our children are. It isn't a bit like I thought it would be; miserable, and saddening. They are all so happy, when, in a way, they have little to be happy about. Mum, if I sound as if I'm preaching, then maybe I am.

Oh! And Vicky is enjoying herself, too. She's never had so many playmates, and I think she's going to grow into a better, less selfish, child through being here. Thanks for everything. Come down and see us sometime, anytime.'

The letter was signed, briefly; *love from us all*, and Margaret felt her heart warm to this new daughter she seemed to have gained.

Previously, she had tolerated Janet because she was Ian's choice and the mother of her granddaughter, but now she felt she might begin to like her for her own sake.

Slowly, she turned to the snaps, unsure what she might find there. But, as Janet had indicated, these weren't unhappy youngsters, and she found herself smiling back into one delighted face after another.

But it wasn't the handicapped children, alone, which brought a tender smile to her lips, but the numerous times Ian, Janet, and Vicky's faces enhanced the scenes. Vicky playing ball with a youth of around twelve. The same young boy waiting to catch her at the bottom of a slide. Ian, with two or three children seemingly hung about him, his own face glowing to match the children's.

And Janet! Margaret felt tears prick her eyes as she turned to the last snap; one of the daughter-in-law she had thought of as cold, carrying a girl of six, pick-a-back fashion, with every appearance of enjoyment.

Sniffing back her tears and smiling

at herself, Margaret put the pictures and letter back into the envelope before placing it carefully in a drawer. She would pay them a visit, just as soon as she could.

Going through to the kitchen she checked that everything was in order for the dinner party. Noting the schedule she'd worked out, and setting the cooker to automatic, before deciding she had time for a long lazy bath.

As she passed through the bedroom her eyes went to the dress she'd bought with this evening in view. It was bronze, and silky, falling in flattering folds over her breasts, the back cut in a deep vee almost to her waist. She knew it suited her slim figure and colouring, and the large, gold stud earrings which Keith had bought her on their tenth wedding anniversary, were the only jewellery it needed.

She smiled, realising that the thought of wearing something that Keith had bought her for such an emotive thing as an anniversary, no longer bothered her. Evidently, she was recovering. Humming softly, she tipped bath salts into the water, laying compatible talc and toilette water ready on the vanity unit, before immersing herself.

It was the cooling water which reminded her that time was passing and she climbed quickly from the bath. Powdered and perfumed, she sat before her dressing table to apply her make-up, recalling, wryly, the smear of lipstick and dab of powder that had been the routine at one time. But, as she slipped the bronze dress over her shoulders, letting it fall in sensuous folds around her body, she knew it was all worth it. She really didn't need to check the effect in her mirror, she knew she looked very attractive.

A blush touched her cheeks, fancying Matthew's admiring eyes on her, as she clipped the earrings into place and added a splash of perfume behind each ear and to her wrists.

"Not bad, old girl! Not bad at all!" she told her reflection. "And, less of the old girl. You're as young as you feel, and right now I feel like a girl of sixteen on her first date."

The smell of cooking greeted her as she closed the bedroom door, and checking that everything was okay, she tipped nuts into a dish and carried them through to the living-room as the doorbell rang.

It was Liz, and she whistled appreciatively as Margaret ushered her in.

"You look fabulous! That dress is something else."

"What, this old thing!" Margaret laughed, delightedly, going to open the door to John.

"I didn't know what the drill was concerning warmings, but I guessed you'd probably have everything you need in the way of nick-nacks, so I brought this," he said, handing Margaret a bottle of wine.

"I didn't expect pressies. Thanks, very much," Margaret stood on tip-toe to kiss John's cheek, and from the hall came Matthew's voice.

"Watch it, John!" He handed Margaret a bunch of flowers and what was, obviously, another bottle. "What does that little lot merit?" he grinned.

In answer, Margaret kissed him on both cheeks, before holding out her hands, welcomingly, to Erica.

"Come in, my dear! I do hope you're not going to be bored. Perhaps I should have suggested you brought a friend. I'm sorry, I didn't think."

"Don't give it another thought, Margaret. Apart from anything else, with the gorgeous smells that are issuing from the kitchen, I rather think I'm going to enjoy myself, even if these two men talk shop all night. You don't know what it is to get a home cooked meal that's really cooked, not flung together, as mine generally are."

"Oh, dear! I hope you're not expecting too much."

"Take no notice of her," Liz butted in. "I've seen the preparations. When do we eat, Maggie?"

"Maggie?" Matthew cocked an enquiring head at the two women. "I didn't know anyone called you that. It suits you."

Margaret blushed, feeling his admiring eyes. "Er . . . help yourselves to drinks, won't you. I'm never very sure when it comes to mixers."

"Dad?" Erica tugged at her father's arm. "Can I give Maggie her present now?"

"But, Erica, your father brought the flowers, and wine."

"It's all right, Margaret, this was Erica's own idea. Okay, bring it in." He turned to Margaret as his daughter fled from the flat. "I hope, well, she seemed to think . . . She knew about Barney," he stuttered.

Margaret held her breath. Surely Matthew hadn't let Erica get her a puppy? Surely, he knew she couldn't have another dog, not yet.

"TARA!" Erica cried, coming back, a small black and white bundle in her arms its mouth opened on a huge pink yawn, its tiny claws stretching as it clutched nervously at Erica's arm.

"A kitten! Oh, Erica, he's sweet."

"She, actually," Matthew said, gravely. "Don't forget to bring her into the surgery in a few months' time."

During the laughter which greeted this piece of advice Margaret carried the kitten through to the kitchen and, tossing some dusters into an empty cardboard box, she placed the tiny animal in it.

"You'll be fine, there," she whispered.

"If you're ready," she said, moving towards the table. "I think we could begin. Just sit anywhere," she suggested, and was gratified to see that John made a beeline for the chair next to Liz's. She had hoped they'd get along, now she saw she needn't have worried.

She took her own place at the head of the table, with Matthew on her right.

"Hot rolls, anyone?"

Before any of her guests could answer the telephone shrilled. "Please," she said, getting to her feet. "I won't be a moment. Just start without me."

Above the babble of talk she gave her number, but, as she recognised the voice at the other end her blood ran cold.

"Ross! Ross, is there anything . . . ?" She got no further.

"It's Tracy!" Her son-in-law's voice was reproachful. "The baby's come. You didn't ring, or anything. Tracy wanted you!"

"And it's ten weeks too soon," he gulped. "They . . . they don't know whether, how it will be . . . Tracy's terribly upset, and she was in dreadful pain . . . "

"Ross, Ross, I'm sorry. Look, is she in hospital . . . Yes, of course she must be. Which? Tell me how to get there. No wonder I couldn't get either of you this morning."

She noted down the directions, uttering platitudes in an effort to comfort the distraught young man. "Tell Tracy I'm on my way, and

. . . tell her I love her."

As she turned from the phone she realised that her guests were looking at her, their chatter stilled by what they had overheard. In seconds, Matthew was beside her, his arm going round her waist.

"We heard," he said. "Get your things, darling. I'll drive you down. Erica, you'll be all right? I'm sure John will see you home."

"Yes, yes, of course, Matthew. Don't worry."

Margaret ran to get a coat and handbag, then stopped, looking at the table as she came back into the room.

"You may as well enjoy the meal. Liz . . . Everything's ready." She turned to her friend.

"Don't worry. I'll see to things here, lock up and so forth. You just get down to Tracy. I'm sure she'll be fine," Liz told Margaret.

Margaret gazed into her face. "I didn't go. I didn't even phone. What sort of a mother am I?"

10

THE sky was darkening, the clouds rising like great banks of smoke from the bright band which spanned the horizon. Margaret shivered. The dress she had plucked from the wardrobe after Ross's call, was a summery one, its short sleeves leaving her arms bare, but the real chill came from deep inside her.

Matthew's eyes turned towards her briefly.

"We'll soon be there," he told her and, reaching behind him, he tugged a sweater from the back seat tossing it into her lap. She struggled to pull it round her shoulders, snuggling into its warmth, her senses conscious of the fact that this was Matthew's sweater. It brought a comfort which wasn't due completely to the Shetland wool. As she smiled her thanks she felt the car surge forward as, in response to the urgency he read in her eyes, he pressed his foot on the accelerator.

"There's going to be a storm," she said, and he nodded.

"Oh, Matthew! I've been so blind," she burst out. "So uncaring. Liz told me. She said I should ring. But I hadn't time! Can you believe that? I hadn't time to find out if my daughter was well. What sort of a mother am I? If anything happens to Tracy, or the baby . . . It won't, will it, Matthew?" Her tone begged him to reassure her, to put everything right so that she could cease torturing herself.

Matthew slowed, fractionally.

"I can't tell you that. You've just got to hang on, hoping, praying. But, Ross didn't say there was any immediate danger, did he? And these days . . . Try not to worry. Everyone will be doing the best they can."

Margaret nodded, but she could take little comfort from his words.

"Ross was angry," she said, quietly.

"Angry?"

"Yes. He said Tracy had wanted me. But . . . she never did, all her life. I don't think she ever asked me for anything. Never relied on me, or her father. But, all the same, I shouldn't have failed her. I should have been there, when she did need me."

"But she didn't tell you, didn't ask for you?"

"No, not in so many words. But she told Keith, at least . . . I think that was the impression he got."

She smiled wryly. "Keith was never the perceptive one. I was the one who did all the worrying. How I've changed! We were having a party," she said, as if Matthew might not know. "My daughter was giving birth, prematurely, and I was having a party!"

"Stop that!" Matthew's words cut through her misery. "There was nothing you could have done, even if you had known. Darling," he went on, his voice gentler. "Even if you feel you have something to blame yourself for, it's doing no good to worry about it now. You're going to need your strength. Don't dissipate it on useless might have beens."

"I'm sorry. I do know you're right, Matthew. But . . . If things go wrong, how will I live with it? Tell me, Matthew. You know. You've gone through something like this. Tell me, please."

The powerful car ate up several yards of motorway whilst Matthew struggled to answer.

Margaret stared through the window, unaware of the passing scenery, her feet pressed to the floor of the vehicle as if she could force it to move even faster, whilst before her eyes flashed a series of pictures.

Tracy as a tiny baby, her mouth opened in a wide, protesting yell. Even that first day she had seemed to reject the world she'd been summoned into. She had protested further whenever Margaret had tried to attend to her, causing her mother to feel gauche and useless. Yet she had coped with Ian! But I couldn't do a thing right with Tracy. Even so young, I suspect she knew what she wanted then, and whatever that was we weren't giving it to her. I wonder how her child is going to behave?

Suddenly Margaret realised that she didn't know whether the baby was a boy or a girl. Ross hadn't said, and she had been too upset to ask.

It might never matter, she thought. If he, she . . . No, I won't think of that. I mustn't!

"Can't we go any faster?" she cried.

Matthew's fingers left the wheel to touch her hands where they twisted in her lap. "I'm doing over seventy."

"I'm sorry. It's just . . . How much further?"

Matthew checked the miles. "Half an hour, with any luck."

"Margaret," he said, abruptly, showing he had been thinking over what she'd asked him earlier. "I wish there was something I could say that would help.

I wish I could tell you how to cope. But I don't know how. I wasn't strong when Alicia died. I wish I could say that I had been, that I had buried my own sorrow for Erica's sake, but I didn't, I wasn't. I went to pieces."

Margaret glanced round at him, her eyes running over the contours of the face she had thought strong. Did it make any difference to her love for him that he had admitted to being human? For that was what he'd just done.

"I let Erica help me," he ground out. "She should have been able to lean on me, but . . . I was the one who did the leaning. Knowing that still hurts. But, you, Margaret, you're strong." He thumped his hand against the steering wheel. "You are! Believe me! You'll cope, whatever you have to face."

Margaret didn't speak, biting her lips, turning to stare through the window again as she felt the pace of the car slacken.

The hospital grounds were quiet, the public car park almost empty.

She scrambled from the car, walking rapidly towards the lighted buildings, forgetting Matthew.

He caught her arm. "Hold on, my dear! We must find where we have to go." His eyes scanned the direction boards. "This way!" He took hold of her hand, comfortingly.

Margaret quickened her pace until even Matthew had to lengthen his stride, their feet echoing as they walked into the quiet of the reception area. Coming to a sudden halt Margaret gazed about her.

"Ross? Matthew, where is he? What's happened?"

"Hush!" Matthew spoke calmly. "He'll be in the . . . ward. Don't they let fathers stay, these days? We'd better ask. Er, Mrs . . . ?" he began, as the young woman behind the desk smiled at them.

"Cunliffe," Margaret supplied. "Her husband, my son-in-law, telephoned. The baby's premature."

Her voice faltered and the woman

behind the desk smiled sympathetically.

"Don't worry! I'll get someone down to talk to you if you'll just go into the waiting-room."

Matthew touched her hand, leading her into the chair lined room.

Two young men were sitting there, apparently absorbed in the posters on the walls, yet when a man in a white coat entered they both sprang to their feet, but he walked towards Margaret.

"Mrs Draycott?" Margaret nodded, and Matthew watched as they moved a few paces away. "Your daughter is quite poorly, Mrs Draycott. We had to do a Caesarean section in the end."

Margaret felt her stomach muscles tighten, recalling Tracy's birth. "But she's going to be all right?" she faltered, and the doctor smiled, noncommittally.

"Of course! She needs rest, that's all. Her husband's with her."

"How is he taking it?" she asked, remembering the gabbled words over the telephone and the nervous pitch of his voice.

The doctor grimaced. "Not too well, I'm afraid. Of course it has been a strain. Tracy's labour began early this morning . . . "

"This morning!" Margaret broke in. "Could I see Ross? Perhaps if I talked to him?"

"I think that's an excellent idea. I'll take you to him. Mr Draycott?" The doctor looked to where Matthew was standing, a few paces away, and Margaret hastened to correct him.

"This isn't my husband. Mr Sayers drove me down here. Matthew! I'm going to talk to Ross. Do you mind?"

"That's all right, my dear. I'll wait here."

Margaret followed the doctor, her thoughts busy. What had started the labour, so early, long before the baby was due? She hurried after the doctor but he had already stopped before a door.

"Don't worry about the tubes and things, they're simply monitoring Tracy's progress, you understand."

Margaret nodded, and he opened the door, motioning her inside.

Ross was sitting by the head of the bed, his eyes fixed on Tracy's white face, his hand holding hers.

"Ross." She spoke softly, but Ross looked up, and Margaret moved closer, taking his free hand. "Oh, Ross! I'm so sorry. Sorry I wasn't here. Sorry about . . . everything."

She was apologising for her apparent lack of thought during the past months, but Ross brushed her words aside.

"She's sick! She was in such pain. I didn't know it would be like that. Is it always so bad? How do you stand it?"

He had risen to his feet, allowing Tracy's hand to slip back on to the cover.

"She is going to be all right, Ross! She's just resting now. She needs to rest. But she'll be fine, in a little while." Mentally, she crossed her fingers. "I wish I'd been here. Ross?" A thought struck her. "How's the baby? Where is the baby? Ross, no one's even told me whether it . . . was a boy or . . . Don't you know,, Ross?"

"A, a girl, I think. Yes, I seem to remember . . .but . . . They took it away. I don't think I even saw it. Tracy was . . . . I wasn't there. I wasn't with her. She'd asked me to be with her. I'd promised! But, they wouldn't let me stay. They came and took Tracy away. I kept asking them to do something, she was so, so . . . But I didn't want them to take her away. They had to operate, they said." He sank back on to the chair. "That's why I can't leave her now. I promised to stay, you see."

"Yes, dear. I understand. But, Tracy will understand, too." Margaret glanced ostentatiously, at her watch. "Ross, the doctor said I mustn't stay long. Wouldn't it be better if we went outside? Just into the corridor? Just so we could talk? They'll know, if she wakes." She nodded to the instruments to which Tracy was connected. "The nurses will know."

Reluctantly Ross allowed her to lead him out into the passage.

"Did they say what had caused the baby to come so soon? Had she been ill?"

Ross shook his head. "I don't think so, well, not ill. She got tired and she was fed up. She didn't like being pregnant. She's always been so . . . such a live wire. You know!"

Yes, Margaret knew, who better. She remembered the way Tracy had spoken that day they'd met for lunch. How she'd complained about not being able to go anywhere.

"Yes, I know," she murmured. "Perhaps it's a good thing the baby did come early. She, she is . . . alive?"

"Yes, yes. I suppose so. They took her; — " he seemed to have difficulty framing the word; — "her to the special baby unit. She was little, tiny . . . I've got to go back. Tracy might want me."

He pushed himself from the wall.

"Ross, did you phone her father? Tracy's father?" she repeated, as Ross stared at her. "You rang me. Did you tell Keith?"

"Oh, Lord! I never thought! Tracy said to call you, — I'd been meaning to, from when we got here, but I was in such a state . . . I'm sorry. And I forgot altogether about Mr Draycott. I'm sorry."

"Don't worry. I'll do it now. Yes, you go back to her, Son." Margaret reached to kiss Ross's cheek. "Go along," she said. "I'll attend to things."

When she found her way back to the waiting-room Matthew came towards her. "How is she? Are you all right?"

She smiled, patting his anxious cheek. "I'm sorry. Were you worried? I've been talking to Ross. He was in a terrible state. I'm not sure he's any better now, but . . ."

She shrugged. "I did my best. Tracy's unconscious. That doctor implied she was simply tired, but, Ross won't leave her," she said, and there was a look of something like envy in her eyes. A look which caused Matthew to pull her into his arms.

"I've got to phone Keith," Margaret said, after a moment, moving gently out of the embrace.

Matthew dropped a shower of coins into her palm. "Have this one on me."

"Thanks!" She looked into his face, hesitantly, and he read her thoughts, moving back to his seat. "I'll be right here."

When a woman's voice answered her, Margaret almost put the phone down, but remembering why she was phoning she asked, "Could I speak to Keith? Keith Draycott?"

"I'm sorry, Keith's not here, just now. Could I take a message, or get him to phone back?"

"Do you know when he'll be in? It is important. Er . . . who am I speaking to, please?"

"Lydia, Lydia Jennings."

"Oh!" Margaret's throat tightened.

But she had to speak to Keith.

"This is Margaret Draycott. We did . . . meet, at the vets."

"Yes, of course! Look, forgive me asking, but is something wrong? You sound anxious. I don't know when Keith will be back, and if it is important, then I'd like to help."

"Thank you. Yes, it is, very important. Tracy, Keith's . . . our daughter, has had her baby. She's not well. It was two months too soon, and they did a Caesarean. Keith would want to be here, I'm sure."

"Of course he would. I'm very sorry, Mrs . . . . Margaret. Look, I think I can contact Keith. I'll do my darnedest, anyway.

"How is the baby? Oh, boy or girl?"

"A little girl. Very little, from what Ross says. She's in the special unit. They haven't said much. To be honest I haven't enquired; there hasn't been time, not really."

"Don't worry, Margaret. Well, of course, you're bound to do that, but

. . . try not to. The little mite can't be too small at seven months, and one hears of babies surviving much more premature than that."

"Thank you," Margaret said, quietly. Though Lydia had only said what anyone would say in the circumstances, coming from her, somehow, it did give Margaret courage. "Thank you," she said again. "And if you could get Keith and tell him where to find Tracy."

She went on to name the hospital in Birmingham and give Lydia precise directions.

"Now, you just leave it with me," Lydia told her. "You get back to your daughter, and Keith will be with you, as soon as possible."

"Thank you. Thank you, for . . . for understanding, Lydia," Margaret said, before replacing the receiver.

As she turned away she was smiling gently. There had been no bitterness in Lydia's voice. Perhaps the time for bitterness was past.

Margaret walked towards the waiting-room, once more, but as she pushed open the door Matthew came towards her, taking her arm and ushering her out into the corridor. Margaret looked up at him, enquiringly but as the sounds of jubilation reached her she understood. How many other babies had been born this day? How many times had fathers laughed and cheered when the news reached them? And how many more might there be before she could leave this place with some feeling of peace?

"There must be somewhere else we can wait," Matthew said. "Perhaps a breath of fresh air would do you good."

Margaret smiled. "Perhaps, but . . . later. I think I'd like to see the baby, if they'll allow me to. She is my granddaughter."

"Of course! Did they say where she was?"

"Some special baby unit. I'll ask."

She found the place, quite easily,

and gazing at the nursery pictures pasted on the windows which lined the corridor, her heart lifted. It looked a happy place, a place where there was hope. Tentatively, she pushed open the door, standing hesitantly just inside it as she saw the glassed in cubicles with their array of incubators. Through the glass walls she could see the monitoring screens, their green tracers moving busily, red warning eyes dulled, but ready to glow brightly. A nurse came towards her.

"I'm Mrs Draycott. My daughter Tracy, Tracy Cunliffe, had a baby earlier today, a little girl. She's premature . . . "

She got no further. "Yes, of course! The Cunliffe baby. And you're Granny. She's holding her own. She . . . Your daughter didn't say what they were going to name the little mite, did she? It's so much nicer if we have a name. We like to get to know our babies. The trouble is, in this place, you just get to love them and they go home. Selfish these parents, always want to take them away from us," she chuckled.

Margaret smiled. "I expect that's what you want, really."

"Would you like to see her? Grand-parents are permitted whenever they want to come in, as are the parents, of course."

"If you're sure I won't be in the way, just for a moment or two. Tracy hasn't regained consciousness yet."

"Mmm! Caesarean, wasn't it? Don't worry! She'll be fine, I've no doubt. Now, if you'll just scrub up and put on a gown."

The young woman showed Margaret to the washbasin and indicated a cupboard with shelves of starchy white hospital gowns.

"Drop the gown in the bin when you come out, won't you? And come round to the desk when you're ready. I'll introduce you to your granddaughter."

As she walked towards the desk a few moments later, a young woman, similarly attired, came from one of the tiny rooms. She smiled at Margaret.

"Two ounces," she cried, clearly unable to restrain herself. "Two whole ounces she's gained. Isn't that wonderful? At this rate she's going to be as fat as a pig."

"I'm happy for you," Margaret told her, but the girl seemed scarcely to hear as she skipped on her way.

With even more eager footsteps after this encounter Margaret followed the nurse who led her to one of a line of incubators.

"Hello, poppet! Here's your Granny come to see you," the nurse said, bending over the crib. "What about waking up and taking a peek for yourself? She looks a nice sort of Granny. Young enough to play games with you, not the sort I had."

All the time she was talking her fingers were checking the apparatus which was wired into the crib and the baby, and Margaret followed her movements, her breath catching in her throat as she saw how small the child's body appeared against the nurse's hands.

"What weight is she?"

"Three pounds. Not bad really, but she's having some difficulty breathing. You see the lungs aren't very pliable at this age. They weren't meant to be in use, just yet, were they, Pet? But, otherwise she's fine, for a prem, of course."

Margaret nodded, and took the stool the younger, woman pulled out for her.

"Talk to her," the nurse suggested. "It helps . . . both of you."

She was gone with a slight smile and Margaret looked down on the tiny figure, splayed out, — like a specimen on a disecting slab, she thought. There was a hand knitted bonnet on her head but that was all the clothing she wore.

"Oh, darling!" she cried silently. "You've just got to get well. You've got to fight, hard. Be like your mum.

She was always a right toughy."

Thoughts of Tracy brought tears to her eyes and she got to her feet.

It might be some time before Tracy could visit her baby but Ross ought to see her. Perhaps it was natural for him to be concerned only for his wife, at the moment, but the baby counted too.

"I'm going to bring your daddy, my sweet. He can't help but love you," she whispered.

Nodding her thanks to the nurses she made her way out.

Matthew slipped his arm round her as she joined him, and she smiled up into his face. "Thanks, Matthew. I don't know what I'd have done without you. It's funny, you know. When Tracy and Ian grew up, I used to think of the time when I'd be a grandparent, long for that time, even. Then, after . . . well, later, and when I started to work for you and John, and my life changed, I changed too. It sounds terrible now, but I wasn't interested in Tracy's baby; not when she was carrying it. It was just something else, something that threatened to pull me back into the old life. Now ... "

She nodded back to the baby unit. "Now, I can't believe I ever felt like that. I know there's Vicky, my son's little girl, but Tracy's my daughter. Perhaps it shouldn't make any difference, but it does. Besides, she's so, so helpless and dependent. I can't believe it myself, but, already I love her."

She laughed, a little dryly. "I expect I'm going to turn into just another boring granny. Will you mind, very much, Matthew?"

"I won't mind at all. And you wouldn't be you if you didn't love the child."

"I've got to get Ross to come down. He needs to see the baby. Oh, I do wish they'd told me .... but I never asked about names." She swallowed, forcing down the misery which threatened to gather again.

"I'll ask Ross if they'd thought of

anything. It won't matter if they want to change it later, but she ought to have a name. Baby Cunliffe, indeed!"

Ross was sitting outside the door of Tracy's room looking lost when Margaret made her way there. For a second her heart skipped a beat but when Ross turned his face to her she saw that nothing terrible had happened.

"There's no change," he said. "She's no worse, they say, simply resting. Apparently people are different. Everyone doesn't come out of it the same way. That doctor said she might be sort of escaping. She doesn't want to wake and learn what's happened, scared of knowing, so her mind won't make her wake. I'm to talk to her, he says. Tell her that the baby's fine. I don't know!" He ended, helplessly.

"But she is, Ross. At least, she's holding her own, as they say. I've just been to see her. She's small but they're looking after her and . . . there's even smaller babies. You've got to see her,

Ross. I'll show you where she is."

"But . . . " Ross looked to the closed door. "What if they finish while I'm away? I must be here to go back to Tracy."

"Ross, didn't you just tell me they want you to talk to her, to tell her about your daughter? How can you do that if you haven't even seen her? You'll be able to tell her how the baby needs her. How lovely she is. That her eyes are blue," she invented. "And that she's got your colouring but Tracy's determined little chin. She has, Ross. She really has."

Gently, Margaret eased him away from the ward, talking all the time of the baby and the others in the unit.

"Did you ever talk of names, Ross? Has Tracy said what she'd like to call your daughter?"

He didn't answer, stopping so suddenly that Margaret was a few paces ahead before she missed him. She turned. Ross was smiling, a look of bemused wonder on his face.

"My daughter! I've got a daughter! It hadn't sunk in. I've only just realised."

He grabbed hold of Margaret as she came back to him, hugging her fiercely, almost swinging her off her feet. "I've got a daughter! Me, Ross Cunliffe. I'm a dad!"

"You certainly are," Margaret laughed, delighted by his reception. "Come along. I'll introduce you to her."

However, Ross's expression changed when he gazed down at the baby's tiny, tube festooned body. Tentatively he put out a finger to touch her hand.

"She's got fingers, and nails! I don't know what I expected, but nothing so well formed, so perfect. Isn't it wonderful?"

"Yes, Ross, it's pretty wonderful. I've got to go now, my dear. I rang Keith. I'm expecting he'll come right down. Have a good look at your daughter, then you'll be able to tell Tracy all about her."

There was no one in the waiting-room when she returned but a nurse told her that her husband had gone down to the coffee bar.

Margaret nodded her thanks, not troubling to correct her. But when she arrived in the coffee bar she saw the girl hadn't been wrong. Keith was there, with Matthew. And, sitting between the two men was Lydia.

How long she stood in the doorway just watching the trio she wasn't sure, but it was soon evident that Lydia was doing most of the talking, her bright head turning from one man to the other.

Panic rose in Margaret as she saw Matthew smile at something Lydia said and she hurried to join them.

"Margaret!" Keith left his place behind the table and held out his arms as she drew near. "How are you? I wish I could have been here earlier."

His hands gripped her shoulders. "Tell me what happened. How is Tracy? And the baby? Is it . . ."

"We've got a granddaughter, Keith.

She's very tiny, and not very strong but, . . . She's like Tracy, a fighter. I told Ross that. I'm sure she's going to be fine. As your mother would have said, she's all the world to grow in."

Her voice broke, and her eyes filled with tears, and, instinctively Keith drew her head down to his shoulder. "Yes, Mother would have said that. And, she was never far wrong."

Matthew cleared his throat. "I'll go and phone, Liz," he said, addressing no one in particular. "I expect she and the others are wondering. Excuse me, won't you?"

He began to walk away and realising this, and how he must be feeling, seeing her with Keith, Margaret stepped towards him.

"Matthew." She took his hand. "Thanks. I hadn't given them a thought. Thanks for thinking about them. Thank you for everything," she dropped her voice to a whisper, and smiling tenderly into his face, added significantly. "You told me I could cope, love. And you were right. I can cope with anything, so long as you're here."

"They'll let you see her, Keith — the baby, I mean." she went on, turning from watching Matthew leave. "Grandparents can go into the unit whenever they like, they said."

"Er, I understand you and Lydia have met?"

"Yes." Margaret moved to stand before Lydia. "It was good of you to get Keith here so quickly."

"Keith's car was in dock, it was best he should use mine. And better still that I should drive. Besides . . . well, I wasn't sure how things were here. You sounded pretty distraught on the phone. I didn't know you had someone with you."

"I'm glad she wasn't alone," Keith said, quietly, and Margaret nodded, unsure how to reply.

The silence might have continued if Ross hadn't burst into the room.

"I've been looking everywhere for

you. Tracy's awake! She's going to be all right. Isn't that great!"

"Oh, Mr . . . Dad, I didn't realise you'd got here. It's going to be quite a gathering of the clans, — I rang Mother and Dad. They should be here soon."

"You can come and see Tracy, both of you, I expect. The doctor said you could just look in. I told her about the baby, like you said, Mum. She was pretty chuffed. Perhaps by the time she's up and able to see herself, the baby might be lots bigger."

"Perhaps," Margaret said, as Matthew came back into the room.

"You got through?"

"Yes, but by the look on your face I wish I'd waited. To tell them the good news."

Margaret laid her cheek against his sleeve. "It's the best news ever. Tracy's awake. And the doctor says we can see her . . . Keith and I."

Matthew patted her hand, drawing away from her. "That's fine! Go ahead."

Margaret turned to Keith and he joined her, walking a little way behind Ross, who was hurrying out of the room. But at the door, Ross stopped.

"Mum, I forgot. When I was telling Tracy about our daughter I remembered what you'd said, about names. And Tracy says she'd like to call her Margaret, after you. Well, aren't you coming?" he called back as Margaret came to an abrupt halt.

"Yes, yes of course! Margaret," she whispered, smiling back at Matthew. "What do you think of that?"

"I always did think it was a nice name. Get along with you, Granny," he chuckled. "And Margaret.

"I'll be here, waiting for you, when you come back. Here or where ever," he added, quietly, their eyes meeting.

And Margaret knew she need never be alone, ever again.